Founder

A Fable

Joseph Phillip Natoli

ISBN: 979-8-218-6063 1-2
LCCN: 2025903565

PART ONE

There is no remembrance of former things,
Nor will there be any remembrance
Of later things yet to be
Among those who come after
Ecclesiastes 1:11

Let me back up the drive-way, say, a couple of hundred feet, to last year, the year the Celtics lost to the Knicks in the Eastern semifinals. That was the year everything in town seemed to be recessioning and a lot of people who earned by the sweat of their brow as they say were just standing around waiting to be re-trained into a service industry where they said you didn't sweat.

That was the summer that things suddenly began to open up for my good friend Frank Coletti. The way Frank put it to me was that things in the scene opened up and then the scene changed. Easy enough to explain he told me when I asked him "What scene?" Little Frankie holding up the crappie he had just pulled out of Brady Lake drops out, I mean vanishes, and another kid, not a kid but a sort of an old runt with long white hair and swollen, clouded eyes like a dead fish - this guy takes my godson little Frankie's place.

Now just the thought of that scene pissed me off because I liked little Frankie.

"That's neither here nor there," Frank senior said to me, shaking his head, so I motioned to Gladys down at the other end of the counter to do us up with some more coffee while I listened and Frank explained.

"There's also too many trees too close to the bog's edge and too many sounds, like a soundtrack from a Tarzan movie."

We watched as Gladys poured us coffee.'

"Sweeney around?" Frank asked her.

She gave him a long look.

"Have you ever seen him in here because I haven't."

When she walked away Frank told me that he had once seen Sweeney.

"He's gone missing?"

Frank nodded.

"Long time."

"And a few other things open up elsewhere on that camping trip Frank tells me so when I get back and tell this to Doc MacGowan, my eye-doctor, Doc says as he shoots a puff of air into my right eye:

"What do you mean, open up elsewhere, Sheriff?"

"I'm there, Frank tells me, little Frankie's there and then everybody is someplace else is what I mean by elsewhere. It's like I switched TV channels but I didn't. I mean somebody else switched them. And little Frankie ain't watching anymore. He ain't on the program. Somebody else is."

"Maybe he got cancelled," Doc says to me and he goes over to his desk, looking for a-pen I guess.

"Or re-scheduled. Frank Coletti is about twenty-four hours away from needing cataract surgery. I'm not surprised he's seeing things open up, as you say."

"Cat Racks my ass. Frank's still hitting the bullseye out at Neelye's Target Range."

Anyway, the next weekend Frank approached his weekly camping trip this way: He was about a foot away from needing reading glasses and that would explain things. Suddenly opening up. '

This wasn't the woods behind anybody's house. You go up north past the town, which is already north of Sameold Bay, and you go back in town. Time, I mean, you go back in time and then you go back to town. I went along with Frank and little Frankie because we had a couple of open murder cases on the books and in some ways the fellow that little Frankie had turned into -- you know, in that bit of scene changing Frank spoke of - fit, more or less, the descriptions we had of a fellow hanging around town the day of the murders, April 23rd, bodies found out behind the Founder Asylum. And I'm the sheriff. I mean I was Founder's sheriff back then.

"I like getting away from it all, don't you Frankie?" Frank said as he pulled little Frankie's pack out of the pickup and handed it to him.

"You work all week and you need a change," Frank said, adjusting little Frankie's pack on his shoulders. Frank had been laid off from pulping wood for the Founder Paper Mill, now defunct, for about three months but with Frank you do things, you say the same words. It takes more than three months or three miles before anybody figures out they don't fit anymore: the words, the things.

"Mom sure as hell isn't going to take me out here," little Frankie said. "And my new Dad's into computers."

"Thinking about stepping into the future with your own personal computer?" I said, knowing full well that he was which was why nobody needed paper any more.

"I think so," little Frankie said, glancing at his Dad.

"Oh, yeah?" Frank said, curious, looking around and then down at his compass. "What say we head off into a different direction? There's a small lake over that way that I fished in with my Dad when I was a kid. I took a helluva pickerel out of it I remember."

The sun was beginning to feel its oats now and Frank took off his jacket and tied it around his waist. About an hour or so later he spied a small, worn trail, barely visible, that wound in and out of brackets and brambles, over pissing creeks and through thorny thickets, under natural passes and over hilly rises, and wound up deceiving us. It ended late in the day, about four o'clock or twenty miles, in the ashes of a campfire and a pair of blackened lacy underpants hanging from a branch. We had no idea where we were and little Frankie looked worn out, his Tee shirt drenched, his head raised high, eyes squinting, dried lips plugging away at an emptyish canteen.

Frank heard a familiar noise in the bushes to his right and he turned, whistling a double beat, pause, double beat as he did so.

Fatima was long and black and not fat but heavily muscled, a cross between a Lab and an Alsatian, alive and not dead although Fatima was Frank's dog that had died in these very same woods when he was about little Frankie's age.

"I told you about her," Frank said, laughing, leaning back and bracing himself so he could meet the dead Fatima's lunge without falling over.

"Maybe your dog had a pup and this is that pup," little Frankie said, his eyes wide, no longer tired. He loved dogs.

"Sure, sure," Frank said over and over as he crouched down and wrestled with the playful Fatima. Boy, had he missed her. For twenty, thirty .... For thirty-one years he had missed her. Too long. So long that when I looked up at little Frankie, I could see the distance.

All of a sudden, I could see Frank in the distance sitting on a rock, taking off a hiking boot, vague, shimmering, on the periphery. I could see Frank the way he was when we were boys together in those same woods. That meant his father had to be some place around here too. I looked around and saw him, the old man, watching us, his eyes bright and shining as if he were still alive. I figured this was "an opening up." I had experience in handling the facts of things as they come.

But when I turned it was the grown-up Frank playing with that dog and he was looking at me.

"Opened up for you, didn't it?" he said, and I nodded. Frank and I didn't need many words between us. I'm always looking for an opening in a case, like who pumped those bodies found out behind the Founder Asylum, or what happened to Frank's old man not too far from here on a camping trip almost forty years ago.

"This dog would have to be the pup of the pup that my dog had," Frank's father said. "It was that long ago, Frankie. No, I think this dog is really my dog, Fatima. Don't you, Jake? Don't you think this is Fatima? Look at her."

I looked down at her, on her side, the eyes full of mischief and play. Yeah, it was her. That was his father, he was himself, and little Frankie in the fade – I mean in the shade - was little Frankie, fading because he hadn't been born yet is what I surmised, thinking on my feet. You get retired, you don't stop thinking on your feet.

Frank pulled the compass out of his pocket for stability and took a reading for going back to the pickup. North northeast. Too late to go that direction that day. We would have to camp there.

"What do you think happened with those things there, Jake?" little Frankie said, pointing with the bundle of dead wood he had gathered to the panties hanging from the branch.

"Reckless camping, I guess," I replied, wondering if this wasn't a good opening to bring up the birds and the bees.

"You know, Frankie, someday you'll say to your Dad, I got a big date this weekend and won't be able to go camping with you."

"1 bet you could tell a real scary story about what happened here," little Frankie said to me. I guess what little Frankie had in mind was my involvement with those weird crimes perpetrated in the vicinity of the Founder Asylum that the *Founder Chronicle* had made much of.

"Let's save it for the campfire," I said, noting that Fatima had disappeared.

Frank looked down at what he was doing: building a fire. I knew Frank. Frank was never scared I tell you but he was scared now. He was too scared to look around. What if his father were sitting cross-legged on the ground just behind him, with Fatima, the world's oldest living dead dog lying beside him? It was far better to build a good fire, heat up the beans, get the coffee going and think about sex. He wasn't thinking about sex but I was and I think we both could use sex to correct failing vision. And a lot of the problems of being out of work.

When the fire was going good, we put up the Eureka tent and stretched out the sleeping bags. Finally, it was too dark out there to see if anybody that shouldn't have been there was there. We sat by the fire and ate the beans. As time wore on and night stretched deeper and closer, the firelight kept making end runs into the darkness, yardage won and then lost, only the cackling keeping the score. It never gets so dark as it gets out in those woods.

"Dad, can I ask you something?"

"Sure," Frank said, pouring himself another cup of coffee.

"Aren't we pretty close to the place your father was killed?"

"That was too long ago to be that close," Frank said. "What I mean to say, Frankie is that I can't remember. We took a wrong turn or we wouldn't be back here at all."

"Mom says you were with him. Out here."

"You think your Mom has a better memory than me, Frankie? Who's the one who got married again? That'll tell you who can remember things and who's good at forgetting them."

"Let's change the subject," I volunteered. "You want to change the subject, little Frankie?"

"Make it scary, Uncle Jake."

"Sure, let me tell you about those panties hanging over there. Someday somebody in panties like that will mean more to you than both your Mom and your Dad. Or camping. And that's just the way things are. You inch forward in your life like on a trail and there ain't no going back. You go from one campsite to another. Day after day, year after year. Mile after mile. Faces wear out, disappear, leaving behind new faces, always facing forward. I don't know why they always face forward except if you notice we've only got faces on one side of our heads and we just gotta go where we're facing."

"You could turn around and go that way," little Frankie piped up but I could tell by the sound of his voice that the dark eeriness was beginning to sink into the kid's very being.

"You'd still be going the way you were facing, little Frankie. See what I mean? It ain't direction, little Frankie. It's falling through on your way there that's scary. And that's what happened to them normal citizens out at the Founder Asylum. They fell through."

"You're new Dad would say they went off-line," Frank said sarcastically. "I heard they're letting out some of those fruitcakes so they can live a normal life with the rest of us normal only thing is they ain't normal. As is that Director they got out there. Birke. Jayzus have you seen that fellar? Never in daylight is what I hear."

"Hell is a camp!" someone from the darkness yelled out just then but I took that to mean "Hello

"We're lost and looking for some help!"

I could see Frank's face by firelight, there and then dark, there and then dark. Like I say we didn't have to say anything. I was ready. I pack a weepon on my belt and one in my boot. Frank gave the come ahead.

"Come ahead," Frank called out, as I stood up and backed away from the fire, leaving Frank and little Frankie huddled there, blankets over their shoulders. Just before the figures of three people emerged out of the darkness, the fire flared up and illumined an empty branch where lately the lacy panties had hung. There were two men and a girl with long blonde hair who came up to the fire. Now I could only see one small figure by the fire, a boy's hand wrapped around Fatima's collar as she snarled at the approaching figures. I rubbed my eyes with my knuckles. Such was opening up again but I was ready.

"Quiet, Fats," my friend Frank as a boy said. Things were opening up again quick and I had my hand on the weepon I always carried just above my wallet pocket. I was also prepared if necessary to drop down, pull the weepon in my boot and exchange fire as needed.

"Waz that, a dog or a wolf?" one of the men asked, who was so tiny I first took him for a kid until I heard the sound of his voice.

"We could use some food and coffee, friend," the other man, who must have been seven feet tall, said. "We left the car this morning to just go off and picnic. Don't ask me how we got lost."

"We'll trade yez for this," the tiny man said, pulling a bottle out of the front of his pants and waving it over the fire. "Jim Beam. Set ya right up for a night under the stars.

Lost or not lost. It don't matter."

I was about to step out of the shadows and say something against the use of alcohol on family camping trips when I realized someone else was standing in the darkness with me. It almost made me pull on him I got so startled but I turned my head slowly and gave him a look see. It was Frank's old man, but he wasn't old and he wasn't dead. He was about the age Frank himself was right then. Or should have been if things hadn't suddenly opened up on us.

"It doesn't help to get drunk if you're lost," Frank's father said but he didn't quite say it like that because he was a pulper, like Frank had been before the big lay-off, wood into paper all his life is what he knew. Nobody knew what had happened to him: went camping with young Frank and Fatima way back then and all that came back was young Frank in deep and timeless shock.

Now Frank's father said: "I got my twelve-year old son here and we're camping and I don't need any drunks spoiling things for us. If you want to stay, give me the bottle."

"Screw you," the twisted little guy with the bottle said, but the other man reached out and grabbed him and shook him up and down and then the bottle fell to the ground and the blonde young girl picked it up and handed it to Frank's father.

"He's just drunk," the girl told him. "He'll be out like a light in another minute. Won't give you any trouble at all in just sixty seconds. He's not even five feet tall. Can we have some coffee now?"

"I'm scared," somebody said to me and there sure enough was little Frankie standing alongside me. "Where's Dad?"

I motioned to the group now squatting around the fire, the three intruders, Frank as a boy and his dead father. I knew I was getting set to make an arrest. There were enough open murders present and past I could question these three about. I was just waiting for things to close up and get back to the way they were. If I kept blinking my eyes, things would get back to normal. Being a sheriff like my father and my grandfather had been before me is a lot like this: hanging around just waiting for things to fall in place so you can go in and make your arrest.

Meanwhile, little Frankie and me stayed in the shadows.

Frank's father wound up giving the tent to the girl and his son while he slept outside by the fire with the two men. Frankie and I crept around to the back of the tent and listened.

Frank was giving his sleeping bag to the girl who took it. In return she said she'd let Frank watch her undress. It was too dark to see much but the fire did run all sorts of crazy patterns on the inside of the tent that made me think something deep and gymnastic was going on in there. Anyway, I needed to see so I raised up and looked through the screened window in the back of the tent.

She was undressing. When she got down to those lacy panties which were not now blackened by the ashes of a dead fire but were whiter than the paleness of her body, I began to put two and two together. Sex and murder were opening up. And I was on the scene. We were going to fill in a couple of holes in the old road of unsolved crimes. If you're Coastal, you won't think such can happen in Founder but it does but mostly it doesn't is true too.

Frank's father must have heard something he didn't like, maybe a violating word she had used, or a sound of ecstasy she had made, but he flew into that tent and ripped out of her hand the panties she was brushing across Frank's mouth as she sprawled on top of Frank. He pulled her out of the tent and as I came around, I saw the panties go out of his hand and fly across the spotlight of the campfire and land nobody knew where until now, years later.

I don't know why we never heard the gunshots, or the sound of Fatima barking her last bark, but now I didn't have time to try and figure it out. It was my chance to find out where they took Frank's father's body.

And so, I followed. I checked my compass in the firelight. North northeast.

"Where you going, Jake?" little Frankie asked as I set out after the figures retreating into the shadows, Frank's father flung over the seven-foot man's back like an unrolled sleeping bag.

But first it was necessary to get the sleeping bag out of my face.

I raised my head and looked over to where young Frankie lay snuggled warmly and safely in his own bag. And Frank was in his right beside him. They were both there. No intruders. No dog. Had I been seeing that story or telling it to Frankie? What Frank said next told me that it wasn't me who had been telling a story but Frank.

"Whatever you do, don't follow me," Frank said. "No part of me is in the future."

"Your father left you because it was his chance," little Frankie said sleepily and then yawned, "it was his chance for something different?"

"It was more like somebody called him and he had to go," Frank said, wondering what that noise was he had heard out there.

"And he yelled back not to follow him?"

"Don't follow me! he yelled back. But I knew that he knew that it was in vain. I mean I was facing forward, watching my father's back disappear into the darkness. You just don't forget your own father that easily."

What Frank said next kind of brought a tear to my eye.

"Time, they say puts a wedge of difference between a son and a father, especially if one of them is gonna rip up his re-training letter when it comes and the other will probably go into a world where they don't pulp trees for paper. Not that I'm a big reader or writer."

Young Frankie took this in slowly like his brain was a boot stuck in mud.

"Did Grandpa get re-trained or murdered?"

"I've been looking for his murderer all my life," I said. "Did you know, little Frankie, that the plant closed right after Mr. Coletti disappeared?"

"Wow," little Frankie said, his voice lacking all enthusiasm or understanding, coming from a long way off, fading into the night. "My new Dad says a maniac must have killed Grandpa. And..."

"And what?" Frank snapped, jarring the kid back to the land of the living.

"And... the plant closed," little Frankie yawned. "And the plant closed when it got too smelly...and information is the future."

"Tell your new Dad that I'm the sheriff and we ain't got any maniacs around here that figure into this case."

"You lost...," little Frankie started to say but Frank cut him off.

"That's enough for one night," Frank said. "We got a big day ahead tomorrow."

When the kid was asleep Frank whispered to me:

"Anything?"

"They disappeared before I could make an arrest."

Frank sighed and then turned and went to sleep.

How long I lay awake I didn't know but then sometime later I was aware that it was sometime later and that I must have crossed a distance of sleep and come out to where I was at that moment. I listened to the dark woods closely. The fire was in its last movements.

Then the noise, footsteps, more than one person, coming toward the camp.

"Hell to the camp!" This time things opened up differently. There was a fight and I got a few shots off, blood and screaming, but no arrests. Things cannot open up forever indiscriminately without someone making an arrest. Frank has faith in that and so do I. We can't just be torn from what we were and left standing around waiting for our time to run out.

And it was dawn, a real dawn and time to go back.

Several miles out of town, Frank took the opportunity to ask young Frankie something.

"I guess you think I'm really acting strange," he said, keeping his eyes on the road.

"I know I was acting pretty weird on this trip," I said. "I mean I know when I'm getting my wires crossed time-wise I mean. Could be the drink. Time's been hanging. Sort of."

"I don't think so," Frankie told us.

"It's not helping me if you see something you think I should watch out for and you don't tell me,"

Frank told his son.

There was a long silence and then Frank reached over and put a hand on his son's knee and repeated his son's name: Frankie? and then sort of perked up and said "Right?"

"Okay, Dad. Little things. Everybody calls me Greg except you and Jake and it's like I'm one person with one identity with Mom and Don and then another person with another identity with you and Jake."

"Gregory wasn't your middle name like your Mom says," Frank replied, trying to keep the steel out of his voice. "You weren't baptized with a middle name. You write Gregory Coletti on anything and you could get arrested for misidentifying. That's saying you are what you ain't."

"I use F. Gregory," little Frankie said.

Frank sighed, shook his head and then gave in.

"Okay, what else?"

"You and Jake had an awful fistfight last night," F. Gregory said.

"We did?" I said, astounded. Why would I be fighting with my good friend Frank?

"And then you were talking in your sleep."

"What I say? Did you catch the words?"

We were driving through town now and were only a few blocks from F. Gregory's home.

"You kept whistling for your old dog and you don't finish your sentences and you start talking to me but you're not really talking to me. You get me nervous because I know you're sitting up in the tent listening for something and I start listening to. I'm scared half the time on these camping trips but I don't tell Mom."

Frank turned the pickup into the long circular drive that took them up to a French style nouveau chateau. A pair of those dogs that look like little greasy mops, Shitzoodles Frank called them came running toward us from behind the house.

"It sounds like shit," Frank said, his hand on the door handle. "It sounds like the end for us, kiddo.

"Frank, Jr. or F. Gregory or whatever. You're going one way and I'm ... I'm in deep shit."

"It's not like you were in the war or something, Dad. A couple of my friends' dads were in Viet-Nam

And . . .

"We ain't anything exceptional, F. Gregory," I told him. "Your dad and me are just trying to get by, make ends meet, meet a fitting end at the right time and not before our time. Meanwhile we're both kind of haunted by what we were. And what happened back then."

F. Gregory just stared at me. I don't think he had a fucking clue as to what I was saying. Which of course I don't blame him. I kind of repeat things and then again, I leave a whole lot out. It's a rough passage sometimes like a hard stool on a cold night.

"You can tell your mother that I ain't waiting around to be retrained," Frank said.

F. Gregory looked at both of us, tears in his eyes.

"She doesn't care anymore, Dad."

"Yeah, she's got a bright future with him," Frank said bitterly.

"It's not that I don't love you both...," F. Gregory said, the tears really coming now. "I know you can't get over your father dying like that..."

"There's your mother," Frank said, nodding toward a slim woman in white shorts and a sweat shirt with the words "Recycle" on it coming toward the pick-up.

"Hey, to be continued, right partner?" I said, giving him a straight jab to the shoulder. "Dry your tears otherwise your mom will think things ain't good with us. Remember kid. Cool Beans. The '90s."

He nodded and got out and started running toward his Mom.

Frank grabbed the kid's stuff and followed. I stayed in the pick-up.

"Sorry about the election, Jake," she yelled to me, waving her hand at me. I wanted to yell back at her that I had been the sheriff in that town for twenty-two years and that no goddamn election was going to put me on a detour. I just yelled back something that made a whole lot more sense:

"Hey, who the hell do you think is being recycled around here?"

Later that day Frank and I scoured the woods near the Founder

Asylum looking for signs, solve a few open murders, make a few arrests, patch a few holes in the back roads of our mental landscapes, break a sweat and keep on moving, hoping things might open up to all our benefit, nervous about being watched from the Facility by Dr. Birke or one of his staff for sign of our last, dying breath, already planning next week's trip back into the woods, straight back, twenty, thirty years of time, whatever the weather.

Dr. Baconey, phenomenological psychotherapist, slugged his Milanta. He didn't wait to see if it would do him any good. He offered the bottle to Birke, the Institute Director, who sat throned behind his desk. They were new to each other. One from the Sore Bum where he studied at the "It's Complicated Clinic" and the other from Supply Chain Management where he studied at the Medellin Cartel.

"Did you know your predecessor put my father in here? Klaus Birke."

"I heard that."

"Psychoanalyst. Said my father was a latent something or other. Not your cup of tea, is it?"

Dr. Baconey took another slug of Milanta.

"The Freudian diagnostic narrative was restricted within a later 19th century Austrian haut bourgeoisie reality frame. That frame has been kicked to the curb."

"The psychonarcotic supply wasn't happening back then. You? Psycho Quant?"

"I put numbers to words. Yes."

Birke squinted at him.

"Punch it up with some second-generation anti-psychotics. We've got an accelerated supply line here."

"If they fit the diagnosis, I will."

Birke laughed.

"The drugs will create the condition. Then you diagnose a condition caused by the drugs that the drugs will cure. Simple profit scheme. Keep this place going."

Baconey pondered that and the fact that Birke had no medical degree whatsoever. But he could keep the drug supply fully operational.

Let me back up several yards to when Birke was interviewing the magician, Tristan Magistus, for the position Baconey eventually got.

It went something like this:

"Threads of affinity? What's that all about? I mean in a clinical setting?

Magistus who sat in the same chair Baconey was now sitting in six years later explained how the world was woven both outside and inside the mind. He let it go at that.

But that was enough to get a corrupted mind like Birke's thinking.

"They got a wrong piece of things in there, right?"

Magistus nodded.

"Treatment is in disclosure," he said, and chugged on his Diet.

"And you've got the bag of tricks, right?"

Magistus nodded.

"I am at the Fifth Level of Ascendance."

He self-puffed at that proclamation. He was a guy clearly that Birke would put on Abiliafonte or Sarahquiff.

"Congrats. That's excellent and all but we're into cutbacks here. We'd have to start you at the entrance salary level. Just for the first seven years."

Magistus stood up and flung his cape over one shoulder. In his mind. It was his tie.

"This in an incredible insult, sir! I could do something now you would regret. I can change your mind with the snap of my fingers. I could…"

"Calm down and swallow this antimanic pill," Birke said pulling a small pill out of his jacket pocket.

I don't know if the Magistus did or not but that ended Magistus and Baconey, much humbler, took the job.

"Why don't you think about taking my father on?," Birke asked Baconey. "Between you and me, he's a royal pain in my ass. He's a souped up 80 hear old sex fiend in here. He's harassing old broads he says are his girlfriends."

"Lingering libido?"

Birke laughed.

"It's lingering out of his pants. Why do these old gobs never zip their fly?"

"Can't you just release him. I mean you're the director here."

Birke laughed again.

"That Freud guy said I was damaged goods. Worse than my father because I got the reins of power in my hands. He meant here in this looney bin."

He paused and leaned forward. Baconey noticed that there were no eye pupils.

"I'm hanging by a thread here, Baconey. They're watching me. Besides, it's a federal rap got my old man in here. I can't upend that."

"What did he do?"

"He never murdered anybody. At least nobody found a body. The son of a bitch is crazy but smart. We treat him like a Vegas High Roller here. If he was in Founder Colonoscopy he'd be already sleeping with the fish. He's a genuine ball buster. You get to hate him soon as you see him."

That made him laugh.

"Don't you have a psychopharmacological course for him?"

Birke shook his head.

"He's had everything. They put him to sleep. When he wakes up, he's him. It's like some demon in him neutralizes the drugs."

When he stopped this round of laughing, Baconey mentioned Williams whom he recommended for release.

"They say this guy Williams is obsessed by a demon. I heard that from the reverend what's his face? Old black guy?"

"Rev. Goodnow. It's not a demon. It's his Sweetheart."

"Touching. She dumped him?"

Baconey shook his head.

"The fact that she only exists in his head is the delusion that has brought and kept him here. I don't think that delusion is dangerous to others."

"You know the kind of love this guy has is a form of mania. Why don't you give him this?"

Birke took a single pill out of his jacket pocket and handed it to Baconey who nodded and put it in his lab coat pocket.

"Okay. Here's the deal. Work on my old man's head. Get him to keep his linger in his pants around the ladies in here and I'll sign off on this nutjob Williams getting released."

"Okay. I'll see if I can enter your father's lifeworld."

"Yeah, you do that," Birke said and laughed. "Just don't get caught in there. Take that pill with you."

The way Abe Fata got sacred mushrooms into the conversation was when the Rev. Goodnow began a detailed mapping of his real estate holdings on the south side of town.

"There was a sacred mushroom sect out there three four hundred years ago," Abe said.

"Before Eden's Bower?" Anthony asked.

"Before Ferris's apple orchard which was there before Eden's," Abe replied. "Amanita muscaria. It's what the Centaurs ate. And their Maenad womenfolk. Senseless rioting, erotic energy, and prophetic sight."

"Oh, my," Anthony said, looking out into the darkness that lay beyond the screening of Harry Powell's back porch. "I cannot keep up with the words. And you know all this lady Ambra Nethra how so?"

"Greek mythology. I'm a Greek. It's in our blood."

'Heathenism before the Bible, Sir!" the Rev. Goodnow boomed. "There was nothing before the biblical account of apples and edens."

"You've got a recipe for these mushrooms, Abe?" former Mayor Harry Powell asked. "Is that it?"

"Amanita Mascara, the sacred mushroom, was taken with animal urine," Abe said. "And that's the part that they've left out for years. No urine. You leave out the urine and there's no out of the body experience. That's when you get back to the true ceremony and things start happening."

"Weird things?" Jake said, opening his eyes and shifting his body in the cushioned wicker chair.

"You get eyes on yourself," Abe said. "And you begin to watch. Quiet. In the dark. Balcony seats."

"I know how that is," Jake said, then laughed.

"I just keep my eyes to myself is what my mother Ambra Nethra told me," Antony told them.

"Man wants to be God," the Rev. said emphatically. "He thinks a mushroom will make him God."

"Yes, but look," Harry interjected, "what if things were in other things like sacred mushrooms? What if you just had to eat these certain things in certain ways and then you'd be more than you were before?"

"That's the mall for you," Antony said. "That's the secret of the New Founder Mall. Things are in other things and those things are in still other things."

"What things are you talking about Antony?" Rev. Goodnow asked, annoyed.

"And everybody's eating these things in every which way," Anthony said. "That's why the mall is so powerful. Lots of people be walking around in it. Round and round just to be inside it like it was where God is."

"That whole section south of town was Jackpine," Jake recalled.

"When you're out of the body you watch other people," Abe said. "And what they do. You see things in a different way."

Jake began to tell them about his out of body experience up at Sameold Lake.

"Dr. Baconey told me that part of myself was trying to split off and leave the rest of me behind."

"For what reason, might I ask?" the Rev. Goodnow asked.

"Poor company, I guess," Jake said, shrugging his shoulders. "I've got low self-esteem after I lost the sheriff election."

"Baconey tell you that?" Rev. Goodnow scoffed. "He's an olive-skinned man don't know the psyche of a white man or a black man so how's he gonna help anybody's mind?"

"What was it like, Jake?" Harry asked. "Seeing your own self outside your own self."

"Well, he was trying to scurry off but I called out to him."

"Who's him?" Antony asked.

"Well, it was me but it was him too if you know what I mean."

"I'm not knowing what anybody means when I get outside that facility."

"You're comfortable is what it is with them bed pans is what it means. The world is more than that, Antony."

Antony gave Rev. Goodnow his best frown.

"Look, this is the point," Abe said impatiently. "Was a mushroom involved here?"

"A mushroom?"

"This is a truly sad way to go into the New Millenium," the Rev. intoned.

"You ate a mushroom?" Abe coaxed Jake.

"Yeah, maybe I did," Jake said. "But I couldn't swear to it. Anyway, there's no real communication between me and him. It's like he doesn't hear me but at the same time he's responding somewhat when I talk. I've got him kind of looking over his shoulder. I think I lost that election because of him."

"You realize of course that him is you?"

Rev. Goodnow asked Jake.

"So, what happened after you ate that Momma Anita?" Abe Fata asked.

"So, I followed him around, listened to the Delphonics, read the *Founder Courier* along with the dude and things like that. Then I'm yawning and falling asleep and when I wake up, I'm right where this guy was and he's me and I feel kind of stupid because now I'm inside this guy who really didn't go around doing anything more than a fruit fly going from one thing to another. I'm not partial to reminders that I'm not the sheriff anymore. Geezer retiree. Totally loser I said to myself. Time is gonna run out on that guy and all his stupid ass dumb ass call it a life but it ain't."

"Oh, my," Anthony said after a long, dark silence. "Sounds like you come down real hard on yourself."

That got Jake mad.

"I tell you it wasn't me this guy."

"You realize that's even worse," Rev Goodnow said. "You're schizophrenic. A border line personality disorder. Don't go near that crazy man Birke. He'll pop one of his pills down your throat to un-manic you."

"Okay, okay," Abe said, jumping up. "Who's gonna try a piece of this?"

"A piece of what?"

"It's sacred mushroom quiche," Abe said, taking something which shined in the invisible rays of a faint moonlight. He unwrapped the aluminum foil.

"You have lost your mind, sir," the Rev. Goodnow said.

"Not me," Jake said, shaking his head. "If I get out again, I don't think I'm coming back. I'll make a run for the border."

They all laughed.

"I'm game," Harry said. "Besides I'm hungry. I'm on a senior citizens reducing diet and I had all of a half grapefruit and a tablespoon of cottage cheese for dinner. I won't turn down anything Abe's cooked."

"How about you, Antony?" Abe said, as he held the quiche out to Antony who helped himself.

"I got one more question," Antony said. "What's it like when things suddenly open up?"

"Yeah, but away from you," Jake said. "I mean one you stays still and the other one goes off along with everything else and you're just watching. I wonder if when we were out in those woods out behind the Founder Asylum whether we could accidentally be breathing in these mushrooms?"

"Breathing them in?" Abe repeated.

"Ask yourselves brothers, what's the real need here?" the Rev. declared. "I mean outside of your wanting to be like God. God is our observer. We aren't his. The Celestial First Order of Observation is the way Rev. Ike put it."

"Think so?" former Sheriff Jake Wilcox asked, looking around former Mayor Harry Powell's darkened back porch.

"Maybe we should identify this mushroom before we eat it," Antony suggested.

"I have one out in the car," Abe said, getting up. "And a mushroom handbook."

When he had gone to the car, Jake began to repeat the tale about a camping trip he took with Frank Coletti when things began to open up for them without them eating any mushrooms. As he was unaware of the Deja Vue no one corrected him out of his respect for his office. They were all used to Jake dragging time back and forth, in and out, round and round like it was blocks of words recuperable like acid reflux.

"Frank's dog, Fatima, has been missing for forty years and so has Frank's father but there they were," Jake said. "We're looking and looking and it's dark but there they are. As close to me as you are now."

"Oh, my," Antony said, clearly frightened by the image of a long dead dog and its long dead owner. "What did they look like?"

"Doesn't Frank drink a bit?" Harry asked.

"Not around Frankie, Jr and he was with us," Jake said. "They looked like they used to look."

"Some kind of time warp," Harry said. "Time is like in layers and these layers can intersect and if you're at a nodal point sort of like caught between a quarter note and a half note then you're hearing is caught going in two different directions. At least that's what that guy they let out was saying over at Sweeney's."

"I don't know," Jake said, shaking his head, as Abe came back onto the porch. "That's hard to believe, this being the '90s and all."

Abe lit the kerosene lamp behind them and brought it over to a small table in the corner of the porch. Next to the light he put down the mushroom in a tissue and an old book. He turned to the proper illustration and they all stared at it and then at the mushroom.

"Amanita muscaera," Harry read. "Deadly poisonous."

"That's it alright," Jake affirmed.

"The sacred mushroom," Abe said.

"Sacred?" the Rev. Goodnow said. "The Lord only is sacred. To him we are in awe. Not a mushroom."

"It looks like it kills you," Abe said, ignoring the prophecy. "But you're really out of your body. And then you return."

"Is this part of that story I been hearing around where Jesus is a mushroom?" Antony sked.

"Jesus was a mushroom?" Rev. Goodnow repeated, astounded. "Did you hear that blasphemy from Baconey?"

"No, it was that stranger talking over at Sweeney's."

"That's right," Abe said. "They said that on Oprah. Jesus was a mushroom. Everyone in his acquaintance took a bite."

Rev. Goodnow banged the arm of his chair with his beer can.

"That's what I'd expect from a man half Muslim and half Jew," Rev. Goodnow screamed at Abe Fata.

"And I don't get what I expect from you either, my friend," Abe snapped back.

"Meaning?"

"Hey, chill out here," Jake said, reaching for his Glock which was no longer on his belt.

"Well, let me ask you," Abe said. "Why are you buying up half the real estate in this town?"

"Why? Can't a black man own real estate? Can't a black man finally stake his claim in this town to this town? Can't a black man say no to the command you must make money for the master and make no money for himself?"

"I heard that on the radio," Antony said. "The stranger was broadcasting from Sweeney's."

"Sure, sure," Abe said, waving one hand in the air. "You want a steak I want a mushroom. But I don't bring up that you're black. What's that got to do with it?"

The Rev. Goodnow stood up.

"I have been staked, sir. My Savior has been staked, sir. My people have been staked, sir. And I am here to say they have all ... I say all ... been reclaimed. Without the services of a mushroom."

He snapped his fingers at the quiche and then stormed off the porch. Harry called after to him but the Rev. paid no heed.

"Oh, my," Antony said. "He's hot."

"It's too bad you brought up the real estate thing, Abe," Harry said.

"Oh, yeah," Abe said. "That's too bad it's supposed to be a secret. I mean is that supposed to be God's work? Buying up foreclosed property?"

"I did my share of evictions in this town," Jake told them, loosening his grip from a gun that wasn't there anymore. He missed it as much almost as he missed his late wife.

"That's who's always watching people," Antony said, pointing to Jake. "The law and the police. You don't have to eat a mushroom to have somebody watching you."

"I ain't the sheriff anymore, Antony," Jake said sadly.

"Oh, n...no," Anthony stuttered and they waited. Finally, he said:

"I don't want that mushroom. I don't want to be looking at myself. I got other people always doing that so why should I? See Antony with his crazy petitions? See Anthony cleaning the memorial plaques downtown? See Antony putting flowers on the graves of the poor? See Antony without a coat in the winter? See Antony sleeping in the park? See Antony's eyes, his skin, his nose, his hair? See Antony not a black man not a white man. See Antony crazy. A crazy man. You know what I tell them. I'm half brown, half white, and three quarters what the Almighty made me."

He paused.

His voice had gotten louder and louder and now it was as if he were hearing himself.

"Oh, my," he said. "I'd better be going. I must have been breathing that mushroom there. Good night, people."

They heard Antony open the front gate and then silence.

"No car," Harry said. "Maybe I should drive him back to the Asylum?"

"He is a walker," Jake told him. "Antony likes to walk."

Harry looked at the bit of quiche in his hand.

"Bad chords," Jake said, putting his beer bottle down.

"Temperamental," Abe said. "You probably want to see how I see you, not how you see you."

"Yeah, you could use a mirror to see yourself," Jake said, "but a mirror can't show you who's looking at you unless you already know they're there and you hold the mirror a certain way."

He yawned.

"Is the way I figure it."

"You retired at just the right time," Abe said after a while, thinking Jake was losing it too fast to be allowed to carry a pistol.

"I didn't retire," Jake said. "I lost the election."

"I didn't mean you, Jake. I meant Harry."

"Did I?" Harry replied.

"A restaurant is something you carry on your back like a turtle with his shell," Abe said. "You want to get out of it but you don't know how. I thought when Sweeney opened his place he'd put me out of business. But it didn't happen. He attracted that half of the town that I don't. We got half each. Just enough to keep us hoping we're gonna get it all."

"I never wanted to get out of being town sheriff," Jake told them.

"Look at it this way," Abe told him. "You're having an out of office experience and no mushroom involved."

Jake grumbled but nobody caught it.

"You got out of office," Harry sang out, "you go out of work, you go out of your career, you go out of your body, you go out of your mind. And then you just go. Bingo! You're gone."

"I hope it ain't permanent me being out of office," Jake responded. "I like looking after people and things. And there's a couple a three weird crimes that were perpetrated while I was sheriff that I'd like to wrap up. Officially I mean."

"They wanted people to think it was deadly poisonous," Abe said, picking up the mushroom and turning it around and around. "If I had your law degree and your experience, Harry, I could do a screenplay about it."

"I could do a hell of a final courtroom scene," Harry replied, blowing the kerosene lantern out.

John Williams didn't ride into Founder on a white donkey or on a turtle's back but he was already a regular at *Sweeney's Right Now Café* at the time we sat on Harry Powell's front porch.

I wasn't born yet but I caught the whole thing as it rode by on an Appaloosa Comet from the Black Eye Galaxy. While you cannot directly "hear" sounds from the past in space because sound cannot travel through the vacuum, you can access visual images from the past by observing light from distant objects in the cosmos, essentially acting like a "time machine" as the light takes time to travel to us; scientists can also translate this data into sound through a process called "sonification" to create an audible representation of cosmic events from the past. In oblivion I caught the rush hour IRT light carrying those passengers seated on that porch. It sounds crazy but it's what it is when what is, isn't anymore.

Signed

John S. Williams, the S for Smith, called Along Came Jones by his closest.

The Bone family has been building in and around town for three generations but their current big spec - the Nouveau Founder Estates just behind the New Founder Mall - is caught in the recessional quagmire."

"Aren't these names just goofy?" Kenny Ramakrishna, formerly Kenny Nickles of the R&B band, *Ana Gezic*, said, putting that morning's *Town Courier* down and looking across the table at his youngest daughter, Pancakes, just six.

"What's recess at frog buyer, Kenny?" Pancakes asked, holding up her doll Patti so she could hear the answer.

"They don't mean anything," Kenny said, shaking his head. "Flushing Toilette Manor. Acrid Maples.Dowagers Bower. Scrub Growth Forest. Road Runner Estates. Goofy. They pick those names out of air like people are going to say 'Wow, I want to live in Coastal Front Condos even though Founder is as close to a coast as Nebraska is. Or they're gonna want to live in the Tar Plantation Estates because it's like Gone Went The Wine or something."

The phone rang and then Eve, Kenny's late wife, called out from upstairs that it was for Kenny. At least, he heard her voice but Eve was long dead but when she was alive, she always called to him like that: "Nickels, honey, it's for you."

It was Kenny's twin brother, Freddy. Kenny read the line from the paper to him. "That was Bullard's place," Freddy told him. "Bullard's Chickens."

"Can you see the Bone family putting up a sign "Bullard's Chickens Estates?"

"Maybe he should of. Maybe they would have sold."

"Eden's Bower was Ferris's apple orchard. Best eating apple in the state. You know Birch Run? I mean that was our best picnic spot."

There was a long pause and Kenny could hear his brother sigh.

"If they stop building them, we stop painting them."

"They can build them," Kenny retorted. "I just want them to stop re-naming the whole goddamn history of this town."

"Which you are familiar with, bro?"

"Sun Bone knows a lot."

"Where did he pick it up? Growing up in Korea?"

"Taiwan, I think. Jake Wilcox. . ."

"Jake? He only knows where he thinks bodies are buried that he thinks were murdered."

"Yeah, otherwise, old Jake ain't thinking. But whatever happened back in the day is like yesterday's wood smoke. You know they trashed Old Man Whipple's quarter mile track out on old route 78 so now they call it Whipple's Shopping Center even though there ain't a Whipple in on the deal."

"Well, jeez," Freddy said exasperated. "I should think so. They were having races on that track before the Civil War. The dead gotta die some time. You know what I mean."

As he said that, he heard Eve moving around upstairs. Doing the bed probably.

So as soon as Freddy said that he wished he hadn't said it.

"You mean the living gotta die some time," Kenny said. "And some one or two or maybe just one don't die at all."

"That's a note I hear, brother, for sure."

For a while they said nothing which was unusual for Kenny but not unusual for Freddy.

Finally, Freddy said:

"Yeah, so now it's a shopping mall and they got an hysterical marker out back with a cardboard facsimile of the judging tower."

Some piece of the road somewhat before this conversation Kenny drove to the outskirts of the town for no reason at all except to give it a look-see and how time had contracted what had been to what Developers had developed it into.

Before he got to the time before there was a mess of building construction sites, there was a time where everything was frozen, waiting for the next step. He drove around a bit. When Kenny got back to the center road, he left the beater and walked a distance, trying to see how big a site this third section of the tract was. It looked about the same as the others until Kenny got to the end of the bulldozed path and saw that it abruptly ended, as if a whistle had blown and the bulldozers had backed up and hadn't returned yet. Beyond the black plastic that had been put up as a barrier on the edge to keep the brush from spreading back on to the cleared land, Kenny could see one or two configurations of land and foliage that looked familiar. This had all been the outskirts of town when he and Freddy were kids. It was in a place like this that they would go out for an overnight, or go berry picking, or biking, or later on take their girls, fighting over who would have the car that night. He couldn't figure out whether the nostalgia was in him or out there or whether it was always in him since the beginning waiting for him to live long enough to feel it. Anyway, something of his mind was in what he was seeing. And of course, he didn't have to search far or deep to see Eve there by a sugar maple. The one they had carved their names into.

On his way home he stopped at the Founder Asylum to see Mrs. Hearder, an old woman whose apartment he had painted a year or so ago. They had become good friends but since then she had been committed by her daughter, Earhart, a prize-winning journalist at the *Founder Courier* who had been going around with Baconey, whether seeing him for her column or socially no one knew.

Alzheimer's had made it impossible for Mrs. Hearder to live alone, pushing through her brain like a cheese worm in a pecorino. In that time when Kenny was doing her apartment, she would ask him fifty times "What time is it, darling?" or "What day is it, darling?" And then finally "Who are you?" So, it wasn't an evil daughter thing in Kenny's mind this "committing." The woman was in her eighties and she needed special care and even though the Founder Asylum sounded like something out of the movie Snake Pit -- now there was a place that needed a name change! -- it seemed like a cross between a rustic resort and a bingo parlor to Kenny. With a dash of something creepy since the weird crimes that had been perpetrated in the vicinity years ago out back.

Kenny found Mrs. Hearder out on the sun porch seated in an old fashioned rocker, her wispy white hair stretched straight back and small sunglasses on. Mrs. Hearder's best friend, Mrs. Woad, occupied a rocker next to her, an open book on her lap.

"Darling," Mrs. Hearder said when she saw Kenny. "How's Flapjack?"

She meant Pancakes but Kenny didn't correct. Correcting whatever Mrs. Hearder said was to him like putting new paint over an unsanded wall. It didn't stick.

"She's six years old," Kenny said. "She's sharing a world with her doll, Patti."

"Oh, just like Mrs. Woad and myself. We share a world, don't we, dear?"

"Absolutely, dear. What world is that?"

"Darling, you're too hard on yourself," Mrs. Hearder replied, reaching out and patting her friend's hand.

"Mrs. Woad and I watch the soaps just to keep our minds alert. I tell her who's that and she tells me how Dr. Slovik got involved with this new nurse and his wife is beginning to suspect."

"I lose track," Mrs. Woad said to Kenny.

"Don't we all," Kenny said, recalling what Mrs. Hearder had told
him about Mrs. Woad:

"Darling, her own husband told me her brain is like a piece of
Swiss cheese with all these holes in it. Perforations of the medulla.
Progressive. She falls in and out of the holes, some are like craters,
so it takes days and others are pea size and you don't even know
she's gone."

This of course Kenny recognized was what, Earhart, had told
him about her mother. Ever since hearing those words Kenny
couldn't look at Mrs. Woad's big round head, almost bald, without
thinking there was a pocked provolone under the hood,

"You too?" Mrs. Woad said, her head shaking palsy like, her eyes
too wide open, Kenny thought, like an amp turned way up just to
be audible.

"Tuesday," Mrs. Hearder said, opening her fist and showing
Kenny a small slip of paper with the word "Tuesday" written on it,
the letters etched and re-etched. She turned the slip over and on the
other side Kenny saw a list of four items, the numbers 1 2 3 4
scrawled and re-scrawled maybe forty times per number Kenny
thought. She wanted to make especially sure she didn't lose her
day.

"Things to be on the lookout for today," Mrs. Hearder said. "I see
these words and I know exactly where I am. When that item is done,
I cross it off. It's perfect except it doesn't work with Mrs. Woad."

"I see "Tuesday" written there but what's a Tuesday?" Mrs. Woad
said, pointing to the slip of paper. "When I don't know where I am,
seeing a slip of paper doesn't help. Last time you were here I said
to myself 'Who is this man?' Your face wasn't a face I had ever seen.
After you left Mrs. Header tells me "Kenny" and I say Kenny but it
doesn't connect with anything."

"But today you recognize me?" Kenny asked.

"Is that a question?"

"The poor dear has a fear of questions. Don't fret, dear. Kenny
doesn't ask questions. He's very accepting of where we are at now."

"Is he?" Mrs. Woad said, looking hopefully at Kenny with
tearing, startling blue eyes.

"Just listening to you two is a trip," Kenny said. "You have such
a great way of saying it all. I mean why don't you tape yourselves
and then play it back when you need to?"

"The doctors did that," Mrs. Hearder said. "She said who's that
voice? Why is she talking to me? I don't know her? I wrote down
her name on the bottom of her photograph and I showed it to her.

Who's that woman she said?"

"I didn't like her face," Mrs. Woad said. "There was something sneaky about her."

"That's really goofy," Kenny said, shaking his head, and taking a small red stone out of his pocket and handing it to Mrs. Hearder.

"For your collection," he told her. "I picked it up over at the Nouveau Founder Estates this morning."

"Am I supposed to do something with that?" Mrs. Hearder said, suddenly full of fear, her hands trembling as she raised a sheet of paper to her face. "It's not here."

She looked up at Kenny, imploring, tears in her eyes. Like a bat out of hell Kenny thought.

The stone had fallen from her hand and Mrs. Woad bent down and picked it up carefully, tenderly as if it were alive. She studied it for a long time while Mrs. Hearder ran a finger up and down along her four-item list.

"Am I supposed to know who this is?" Mrs. Woad finally said to Kenny.

"In New England, stone walls last a couple of hundred years," Kenny said, immediately thinking how goofy what he was saying sounded. "Before the Civil War and all."

"Oh," both ladies exclaimed at the same time, staring at the red stone.

Kenny had seen photographs of both women when they were young. Seeing those photos was the reason he had no religion with a book, a building, and personnel attached. There was no worthwhile god who would allow beautiful women to grow old and die.

"Mrs. Kenny is dead, isn't she, Kenny? Mrs. Hearder once asked him. "I mean of course she is but how did she die."

"Maybe he doesn't want to talk about it, dear," Mrs. Woad told her dear friend.

"Nevertheless, I think we should arrange a Celebration of Life for her. Can you get all her friends to attend, Kenny?"

He forgot what he told them and he knew now they had forgotten all about a Celebration of Life but had gone on or more precisely into the moment.

Dr. Baconey handed a wallet to Williams as soon as Williams got into the Asylum van.

"Some get you going money until you get paid."

Williams nodded and put the wallet into a back pocket. He was wearing a respectable business suit from Goodwill. Williams was a lanky six foot plus and both ankles and wrists were visible.

"Let me construct a life sketch you can draw upon," Baconey said, pulling up to the venerable Founder Hotel, a landmark popular with visitors to Founder.

He put together the vita just that morning.

"You were unfit to serve in the Army because of bad feet. You used that time to become a doctor. Your father didn't move down the block to live with a tart. He just died at home when you were young."

Baconey hesitated.

"You don't have a medical degree, do you?"

Williams shook his head.

"No need to worry. I've set up several interviews for you. Emphasizing your unique talents."

He studied Williams's profile. Firm jawline, nose under control, no bulging in his eyes, skin a trifle pale. Mesomorphic body type.

"You don't speak languages other than English, do you?"

Williams thought about that.

"I think I did. On some occasions. I made responses in dining establishments."

"Excellent. By any chance might have you worked in those establishments?"

"I might have."

"Excellent. Do you think you could be a bit more precise in shaving?"

"I think so," Williams said nodding.

"Always get a clean, precise shave. At least while you're staying here at the Founder."

Williams saw a four-story red brick building with a renovated front. An American flag poked out of its forehead half way up and a small brass plaque with the words "The Founder" was stuck on the bricks to the right of cathedral size doors.

Baconey got out of the car, up the step and went inside. He came out with Antony wearing a bright red jacket.

"Antony, this is Mr. John Williams who will be staying here for a few days. John this is Antony, the Founder's man of all jobs."

"Oh, I don't think so," Antony said, first day on the job former

Mayor Harry Powell had set him up with.

Antony took the small bag Baconey handed him and the three entered the hotel. The lobby was impressive in shadows, antique furnishings, scattered Oriental rugs and a birdcage elevator in one corner.

"Excellent," Baconey said, shaking Williams's hand and reminding him of next day's dinner at eight.

"You're a new man, John. Don't forget."

With that Baconey nodded and rushed out of the Founder.

Antony and Williams stood there looking at each other.

"You been up at the Asylum for a while, ain't you? Cause I seen you there. I got the bed pan job over der."

Williams stared at him blankly.

"I'm working here now to pay the nut," Antony said. 'It's one of my "Yowza' jobs. I got a degree from Yale."

"I'm a new man," Williams replied, nodding

"Then I'll call you Adam."

Antony nodded. He never missed a beat with whatever the inmates said.

"I heard that," he told Williams. "We need new mens in Founder. And that's a fact. New man be just the thing. I'm from Columbus, Georgia myself. By way of Lennox Avenue."

The birdcage took them to the top floor and after they entered the fourth door down the hall on the right, Williams asked Antony who The Founder was.

Antony leaned on the dresser and lit a cigarette.

"The Founder? That goes way, way back before the country was settled. It's mentioned in Genesis. But I know couple three things. The Founder didn't have no color to his face. And he wasn't no woman. And he had truckloads of money."

Antony flipped ashes on the worn rug and worked them in with his boot.

"And then he did something to make folks call him The Founder. Which I don't know what all. You with me so far?"

He held out a crushed pack of non-filter Camels. Williams took one and Antony snapped a light out of nowhere and lit him up. Williams sat on the bed and smoked. Antony leaned and smoked.

"You thinking The Founder up there in the clouds, I'm thinking."

"The Founder," Williams repeated.

"The Founder ain't no Creator," Antony said, laughing. "He found what you got here. And he took it and he took a lot. He no more than a thief, the Founder is. And the Creator? He didn't make the world to be shared. He made it be taken by thieves kicking and hitting and killing each other saying who owned what first."

"I love someone I wish I could find," Williams said without any tonal affect.

"Say what?" Antony said, laying William's pack on the bed and opening it.

"I mean I don't dislike the Creator the way you do. Or at all. Because he created my fair Eve. There is nothing that Is not perfect and beautiful in that."

When Antony heard that he remembered that there was an inmate in the Asylum who was looking for someone he called his sweetheart.

"She ain't looking for you, is she brother?" Antony said, taking a few morsels of Amanita out of his service jacket and popping some. He offered some to Williams who took and ate them.

"I don't know if she'll find me here. Everything about me is new"

"She be looking for the old you."

"He never met her either."

Antony felt that called for more Amanita which he popped.

"We can just put a reach out in the *Chronicle*. What's this sweetheart's name?"

"Eve. My fair Eve. I think it would be Eve."

"Oh, my," Antony exclaimed studying this honkey lunatic who had himself split right down the middle. He didn't know why but somehow the town seemed to draw lunatics the way cone flowers drew bees.

"I got some friends living on the edge of their minds just like you is. I can introduce you. You gonna need a support group."

"I had friends at the Asylum," Willams told him.

"I seen'em," Antony said. "Best forget about them."

"And the whole place was full of toys," Freddy said, coming down from the ladder. "I mean they were falling out of the closet."

"Hey, look who's driving a big-ass car," Kenny said. "The Woad Warrior."

"You been out to Sun Bone's villa?" Woad said getting out of the 'cherry red Caddy and slamming the door.

"I was just telling Kenny that Son's got every conceivable toy,"

Freddy said.

Woad nodded.

"The cherry's Sonny's," he said, pointing to the Caddy. "He's driving a LamB, now."

"Sun spoils that kid," Kenny said, bending down to look more closely at a rhododendron.

"You got to paint his place before the weekend," Woad said, avoiding the question. "He's got a big fest on for Saturday night."

"I'll go over there tonight and cut it in," Freddy said, going up the ladder once again. "Kenny can roll most of it off tomorrow. Don't worry. We'll get it."

"No worries on me. You into gardening now, Kenny?" Woad said.

"This is an English roseum rhodie," Kenny said, getting up and pointing to the rhododendron "She blooms with big pink flowers that cut into the leaf. I mean it's an effect. Kind of goofy though the way it blooms different every year."

"What's it gonna be?" Freddy called down from the peak about forty feet above their heads. "Sunny and Son estates?"

"The old man's a sheik," Woad said going back to the Caddy.

"He ain't no sheik. The Bones are Asian far east or southeast and so on," Kenny called out. "Probably Singaporean."

"Like in Star Drawers," Woad said and then jumped into the cherry red, waved and backed down the driveway and drove off.

Later that night Freddy called Kenny from Sun's condo and told him to come on over.

"Sonny's here. He shows up and he's talking my ear off. The kid's confusion drives me nuts."

"Yeah, he doesn't touch ground. I'll have to bring Pancakes. Eve's out with friends."

"Okay, bro," Freddy said. He knew Kenny had been in to see Baconey for a consult but nothing had come of it.

"Whew, it smells of paint," Pancakes said to Kenny when they showed up.

"We can put some ice cream on top of that," Sonny said. "For the sake of your nose."

They both laughed. The six year old and the twenty year old shared a moment.

"Just a little, Sonny," Kenny said. "She already had her sweet for the night."

Kenny started to roll the ceiling where his brother had already cut in. Sonny and Pancakes sat on the floor eating ice cream.

"My father says you have a lot of toys," Pancakes said.

"Toys?" Sonny said. "I don't think so."

"I'm six and three halves. How old are you?"

"I'll be twenty-one someday. Maybe."

"Goofy," Kenny said to Pancakes. "Not your kind of toys. Sonny's got cars, planes, boats, and surround sound."

"Ah," Sonny exclaimed. "I am a member of the Asstocracy."

"Royal blood?" Kenny said. "I do that with bulbs and flowers. Take a look at the rhodies in this catalogue. Mine are like the hip version of these. It's like they're Amazonian."

"It's the bog," Freddy told them.

"Like the bog, right?" Sonny asked, eyes wide open.

"Yeah," Kenny said, taking a folded catalog out of his back pocket and handed it to Sonny who opened it to the first page.

"You could get these six babies here for only $29.95," Kenny said, taking the catalog from Sunny and turning to a page with color photos of six different varieties of rhododendron.

Sonny looked at the page and then at Kenny.

"You want to buy this?" he asked.

"I would but I'm short this month," Kenny said, yawning.

"Use your plastic," Sonny advised. "That's what I do. I'm thinking of getting some crypt."

"What's that? You been grave digging, Sonny? Anway, mine's been invalidated,"

He took the empty ice cream dish from Pancakes.

"I got a line of credit at Fata's Closet though. I've been shopping a trap door powder blue shirt.

"You know who Jolly Joan is?" Pancakes said to Sonny.

"Jolly Joan? Who is that?" Sonny said, shaking his head.

"She makes a cheesecake get thick," Pancakes told him.

Sonny looked quizzically at Kenny who told him not to pay attention to her because she was goofy.

Around eight the next evening when Kenny was watering his lawn and Pancakes was biking up and down the driveway, Sonny drove up in a Lamborghini.

"Jolly Joan," Sonny called out to Pancakes and she shook her head and biked off furiously.

Kenny showed Sunny around his garden, pointing out the notables, including his rhodies.

"Water them deep once a week the first season," Kenny said.

"And then let Nature take care of them. Of course, these babies do look a bit unnatural. I mean their size and colors and all. Amazonian."

They were drinking coffee on the back veranda when Sonny asked what kind of future could a young scion from Founder have?

Kenny admitted he had no advice for scions but he recommended a kid of 19 with a shitload of funding and a Lamborghini should get himself as much tail as he could manage.

Sonny thought about that.

"You should get yourself a Gibson too," Freddy advised.

"I want to go back to Denver," Sonny said. "I graduate from the University of Phoenix in a few years. I have a girlfriend there. Maybe not."

"We played out there years ago," Kenny said. "We knew everybody."

"I saw a goofy man talking to Old Sun," Pancakes said, taking her doll Patti out of the basket on her bike and showing it to Sonny.

She threw Patti at Sonny and then raced up the drive on her bike.

"Who's she talking about?" Kenny asked.

"Old Sun hired some guy on faith."

"A preacher?"

"No. Maybe. What exactly is a preacher?"

"You ever hear old Rev. Goodnow at the Some Day Eventual Holiness Apocalypse church?" Freddy asked. "Maybe I got that name wrong. Anyway, it's literally across the street from Most Holy Redeemer To Come."

Sonny shook his head.

"I'm a Scientists' Witness. Maybe. Sciologist."

"Is that a Buddhist thing?" Kenny asked.

"I don't think so. Maybe. It's more like a drugs thing."

"Maybe your old man could hire Freddy and me? You know just on faith? We're not just house painters you know. People get pipe cast. It's goofy."

"It could be so," Sonny said, nodding. "Maybe. Old Sun hired this guy as a favor for Baconey. A loose nut my father said Baconey released who needs a job. He speaks Mandarin so Old Sun hired him. Maybe Cantonese. Also. Maybe Taiwanese most likely. I think Old Sun speaks Tagalong. Maybe."

"You speak any of those, Sonny?" Freddy called down.

"Maybe. I think if I hear it, I'm ok. It's in the blood, right?""

"That's unusual for an Asylum guy to speak all those languages," Kenny observed.

"Unusual is the door there, bro," Freddy reminded him.

The doorbell rang and Kenny went to answer it.

"My car broke down and I need twenty bucks to get it towed and stuff," the young girl at the front door said as soon as she saw Kenny.

"You don't have a car, Lucy. Did you see Pancakes out there?"

"Your nose is going to fall off," Pancakes said, rushing up with a skid.

"As Pinochle's would, right?" Sonny said, happily.

Pancakes shook her head.

"Who's Pinochle?"

"Whose LamB is that?" Lucy said, pointing to Sonny's Lamborghini.

"She makes a big long line of chalk on top of the TV and then sucks it in with her nose," Pancakes said pointing at Lucy.

"She's just talking goofy," Kenny explained.

"Maybe I could borrow this car just until I get a driver's license," Lucy said, making her eyes go wide and looking at Sonny.

"That is a definite no," Sonny told her.

"I would drive extra careful," Lucy pleaded.

"Well, maybe in that case," Sonny said.

"Bro, she doesn't have a license," Freddy called out. "She's like 12."

The news seemed to shock Sonny, who now wondered how old his girlfriend in Omaha was if right here Lucy looked older than 12. Maybe 18 like his girlfriend. Or maybe she was twelve also?

"I don't think we should talk anymore," Sonny said to Lucy who giggled.

"Pancakes, take Patti and go for a bike ride," Kenny said to Pancakes who was staring at Lucy. Lucy had been Pancakes baby seater for a couple three times until the klepto report.

Kenny was undecided in his heart whether being around Lucy Powell was good or not good for Pancakes. In some ways, Lucy came from a good family, showered, combed her hair and so on but she was goofy. Plus, she lied all the time, told real whoppers about everybody and was a klepto. Her grandfather, former Mayor Harry, had so far kept her juve record sealed. She didn't go to school regularly and played Huckleberry Finley to the tee.

Pancakes told him she and Patti had already gone for a ride so Kenny told her to go in the house and get ready for bed.

"You can listen to one of your Mom's bedtime stories," Kenny said. That thought interested Pancakes so she took Patti and headed for the front door.

"Eve read some kid's stories on cassettes," Kenny explained. "To play when she …she wasn't home."

Pancakes had paused and was listening.

"Okay, Patti," she said, fussing with her doll. "You're going back in ICU so I can flop you."

"Good night, Jolly Joan," Sonny called out but Pancakes didn't turn around.

"I'm very foreign for her," Sonny said, shrugging his shoulders.

"She's just acting goofy," Kenny said, probing the soil at the base of a rhodie.

"I know about culture shock" Sonny said. "You get close to the natives though and bingo the shock is gone just like that. They call it stimulating. Do you think I give off a native vibe? Maybe."

"Frost will do that to Rhodies," Kenny said, looking up at them. "Shock'em just like that. Although I have to admit the weather doesn't seem to affect these babies. They'll bloom in the snow."

He snapped his fingers.

"The Woad Warrior says it will soon be too hot for flowers."

"He's full of shit," Lucy said. "How about the LamB? I'd take good care of it. You ask anybody if I don't take good care of things."

"I don't think so," Sonny said, laughing. "Maybe."

Lucy thought about that.

"You know, anybody steal that LamB would have to take it out of town quick or sell it quick."

They all stared at Lucy.

"You've got a buyer lined up?" Freddy asked.

She giggled.

"That's for me to know."

"Hey, you think Woad is stealing from my Dad?" Sonny asked.

"The Woad Warrior? What would he be stealing? Squirrels? He's happy living in the woods. The man sleeps in trees. You water these guys hard and then no more until the Spring. That's proper care."

"What?" Lucy asked Kenny, feeling dazed.

"The Rhododendrons, goofy. I'm holding water back from them now. You know, I don't think those plants need water or sun."

"Yeah, that's weird," Lucy said. "Maybe they're from a planet that doesn't need water or sun and some seeds got swept on a comet and the comet . . ."

"You gotta go," Kenny told her.

Sonny nodded. He had this opinion of Lucy that her brains had been rattled when the town was flooded and hit with seven tornadoes in one day. Maybe it was six tornadoes.

"I got to split," Sonny said. "I guess I could hang though."

And he left.

"You think that young brother has any brains, bro?" Freddy asked Kenny as they were both getting their gear together.

"Sonny? Maybe he'll grow into them."

"Maybe."

A couple of weeks later Kenny and Freddy were painting the outside of Abe Fata's private dwelling set back behind his café. The hysterical district part of town Kenny called it. Mr. Fata stood below them watching.

"I'd put anything in an aged urn," he called up to them. "Anything."

"Even a rhodie?" Kenny called down.

"A rhodie?"

"A rhododendron. You gotta set those babies into mother earth."

"I wouldn't have one," Mr. Fata sneered. "Do you see one on my property?"

Kenny scanned the domain from his high ladder perch.

"Poor welcoming," he said, shaking his head. "I have one I could give you. Just ready to be transplanted."

"Where do you get all these old pots," Freddy yelled down. "They're huge."

"Mike Woad keeps an eye out for me," Mr. Fata said. "They rise up now and then out of the old bog. He's got a treasure spot in there. Avoid taxes. You see that one over there? My ashes will go into that one."

"Ashes are too alkaline for rhodies," Kenny said disapprovingly.

"Who's talking about goddamn rhodies? I'm talking about my final resting place."

"They'll put you in the walk in cooler at your café," Kenny told him.

Before Abe could reply Sonny's LamB with a damaged front bumper wheeled into the drive.

"My father says I can go back to Tucson next week! Maybe."

"That's great, Sonny," Kenny said, going down the ladder. "I got a rhodie I want you to take so you can give to your girlfriend."

"My girlfriend? Oh, yeah. She lives in Denver. I think she wants the car though."

"Well, give it to her," Kenny told him. "You give a beautiful lady anything she wants."

"I don't think so. Maybe. I'll miss you guys It's been a crazy summer. I want to give this to Jolly Joan. One of the construction guys netted it out of the bog. It's Aunt Luvian somebody said."

He took something out of his pocket and handed it to Kenny.

"What's the story on the bumper?' Freddy asked.

Sunny shook his head.

"Lucy Powell. They chased her and she drove it into a tree."

"That girl is in motion," Freddy said.

"I wonder if Old Sun saw that bumper," Kenny said, when Sonny had driven off.

"I like Dahlias," Abe screamed at them and then went into the house.

"She liked Dahlias too, didn't she? Eve," Freddy asked his brother.

"She does. But you've got to dig those guys up in the Fall then bury them again in the Spring. And they come back to life late in the summer. I don't like the waiting."

"I hear you, bro. What did he want you to give to Pancakes?"

"This," Kenny said.

It was a red stone.

"Aunt Luvian. I think he meant antediluvian. Before the flood."

"And so it might be," Freddy said, looking at it.

"I thought I gave that to Mrs. Hearder."

"Could be two of them," Freddy said and they both laughed.

Earhart Hearder went over to the phone booth at the *Weigh Anchor Pub* and called Mike Woad.

He was supposed to meet her there at just that time but he was late. She hadn't expected him to be early or even on time but she knew he'd show up. She had been in kindergarten with Woad, that's how far back they went. She had promised herself to stop running to Woad but in the final analysis, Woad was a convenience in her life. Her go-to guy although their romance had ended at the Founder High Senior Prom ten years before. She had gone to study journalism at Columbia and he had gone…No where. Or, to be precise in reportage, the woods surrounding the town.

She came back to Founder to take care of her mother, which now did not amount to much since her mother had gone into the *Sugar*

Maple Home for the Aged and Infirm. If she had just come back as a professional journalist, things might have worked out. But she came back full blown Manhattan. There was no Met Museum of Art or Off Broadway plays or every ethnic cuisine you could imagine, or quaint books stores and galleries to browse.

Short of it, she found Founder to be a place you'd expect to find with a name like Founder. Woad hadn't changed but just become more Woad, more Loser living in the woods. That was harsh. He became something that didn't fit in her life. Their only connection now seemed to be the strong bond their mothers had keeping each other alive at the asylum Woad said was falsely named as there were no sugar maples in the fossil forest surrounding the town. Their Mums had been planning her marriage to Mike for years. That seemed to have vanished from their memory banks, thank God.

She was at the bar when he came in, seeing her, waving and coming over. He had a wool lumberjack shirt out of his bulky cords pushed into untied timbos. He was looking more like an unmade kingsize bed every time she saw him.

He pecked her on the cheek.

She rubbed her cheek.

"Stubble is not good. Can't you either shave clean or grow a full beard?"

He gave her a smile.

"While I wouldn't change a hair of you. You're too perfect. Especially when you're a wise ass. What did you want to see me about? The ladies get in trouble?"

He ordered a beer.

The bartender, Further Fata, reminded him that he needed to attend to his tab.

Woad immediately objected to the reminder in public.

"You know, Further, you're a surly son of a bitch. Just lay one more beer on it and whatever the town's star reporter is drinking."

Further poured and pushed the mug to Woad, slopping beer.

"Last one till you pay up, Woad."

Earhart said nothing. She knew she'd be paying that tab. It would be worth it if she could get something from Woad she could use for her story.

"They're doing fine. Your mother worries about you."

Woad sipped his beer.

"Her mind needs a focus. I'm alright with that. If she wasn't worrying about me, she'd be worrying about how many angels make a pin."

"Your mother had this idea you should make something of yourself."

"Don't go high horse on me, Miss Star Reporter. I'm living the way I want to live."

She gave it up.

"Look, you living in the woods and out by the bog is not my huckleberry here. But I want an assist on figuring out one or two things that have come to light."

"Such as?"

"Hallucinations. People are seeing things out there. And people long since dead."

Woad laughed.

"I wouldn't pay too much attention to old Jake Wilcox. He thinks he's solving some murders that were committed out there years ago. When he was sheriff."

"Were they?"

"The murders? Before you and I were born. No story there. What else you got?"

"Have you seen anything of that Asylum patient who broke out? They say he's hiding somewhere in there. You know your home turf."

She signaled the bartender who came over and poured vodka.

"Did you hear that, Further?" Woad asked. "Earhart here thinks I'm harboring an escaped Louie out at my place?"

"You have a place?" Further asked, dryly. "I thought since you live up in the trees you had escaped from someplace."

"Yeah, I'm wanted. You should try to arrest me so I can break your neck."

"Why, don't you drink up and take off. You got a bog smell."

Woad lifted off his stool and reached for Further.

Earhart grabbed his arm.

"I want to go."

Woad turned and looked at her. He smiled.

"And I came here all peaceable like. Am I not a man of peace, Further?"

Further closed his eyes and lowered his head.

Earhart led Woad to a table in the back. She needed more for her story but dealing with Woad was like dealing with a Neanderthal.

"Do you know why Further works here and not at his father's diner?"

"He thinks he can pick up more ladies as a bartender than as a hamburger flipper?" Woad asked.

They heard Further's voice, angry, and when they looked, they saw Lucy Powell all made up and dressed up trying to look 21 and Further was ordering her to get out.

"Are we finished here?" Woad asked Earhart. "Jake and his murderers. Escaped Louie from the asylum. Got your story?"

"Almost," she said, trying not to laugh. It was so easy to rock Woad's world. She guessed it was because he was not used to the give and take of normal human interaction. He spent more time with the squirrels and chipmunks and they didn't talk back. Fact was, no one knew what the woods' attraction was with him. He said he liked to commune with Nature. She thought it was because there were no people in there he could fight with.

"Have you ever come upon any clues or signs of who The Founder was? Out there."

"Yeah, I found the cave he used to live in before he came to town and opened the hotel. That was way after He created the world."

Earhart seriously thought about that even though Woad was smirking. She had punched and slapped him more than once back then but he came at her laughing. If she didn't know he was smart, she'd think he was a happy idiot, not a useful one. He was clever. He was on the Spectrum before anyone knew there was a Spectrum.

"Sun Bone showed me some rocks his men had dug up that had some carvings on them. I sent them to the U for an examination. They glow."

"Radioactive."

"He was probably a slave holder," Earhart said, musing.

"Who?"

"The Founder. The whole town is built on slave quarters."

"Yeah. And they're built on something much, much older than that."

"Animus Mundi?"

Woad laughed.

"Come on. You're spooked. Your thinking runs after some crazy feelings you get."

She couldn't resist.

"That's why I got over you. Okay. I have this feeling that whatever was past here is affecting people. Kind of breaking through."

"I saw that movie. Don't you remember? We both went."

"No, I don't. It was a thousand movies. I have to go. Just do me a favor and tell me if anything at all in line with what I'm thinking goes on out there."

"Sure. I'll keep an eye out for the crazy to match your crazy thinking. Still seeing the Sigmund?"

"Baconey? Why? And yes, I run into him. Is that a concern of yours?"

"Me Tarzan. You Jane."

Instead of answering, she walked away.

Woad went after her and stopped her out front.

"You might be interested in this guy working for Bone now," he told her.

"And why? Who is he?"

"Ask Baconey. He let him out of the Asylum. You know Bone is always looking for his Black Swans, the people who have revolutionary ideas."

"Yeah, the dangerous crackpots."

"Anyway, this guy is looking for his sweetheart. Eve."

"So?"

"Eve. Wasn't she before the Common Era?"

Director Leonard Birke had taken to playing chess with Dennis Moran, a voluntary commitment patient, who had had the kind of fascinating life that Birke's own supply change management expertise had not provided.

According to what Moran told him, he, Moran, had had truly breathtaking adventures all over the world, almost all of them dangerous and replete with exotic romance. He occasionally did spy work for unstable governments and had to retreat to various safe houses as a consequence. He explained that his presence in Founder Asylum was just such an occasion. According to Moran, he hadn't come to the asylum for mental health reasons but only as a calming respite from his life on the edge.

According to Baconey, Moran was a rare case of a psychopath rooted in sociopathy. Or, a sociopath rooted in a psychopath. A double threat to homeowners whose total detachment from any human affect had led to dealing with humans the way fox dealt with chickens.

Birke laughingly dismissed Baconey's diagnoses based on the results of The SOOT test: self, others, objects and time. Birke himself read Moran's responses: Self: "I got mine" Others: "You get yours." Objects: "Women. Time: "Get it while you can." The exact responses

Birke himself had given. Sadly, after Moran had violated Asylum rules as well as several inmates, sending a few to emergency medical care, he had been reassigned from voluntary commitment to criminally insane. Birke went along with it to shut Baconey up. The Voluntaries and the Criminally Insane were on the same drugs.

Moran was a challenging chess player; devious, totally unexpected moves calculated some ten or fifteen moves in advance. This evening, Moran was satisfying Birke's curiosity about an Amazonian pigmy tribe and the nubile Moran had married.

"Maltesia tells me only gods have one blue eye and one black one which is what I got," Moran said as Birke reached across the board to put Moran's king into check with his bishop. Moran struck him on the top of the head with his boot. As Birke lay moaning with his head on top of the board, Moran removed his clothes and put them on. He took Birke's keys out of a jacket pocket and then went out the door. He locked it behind him. In a few minutes, he was backing Birke's jeep out of the parking lot.

It's dark now, close to midnight and raining. Birke is on foot. He sees this majestic old building and it draws him. The *Founder Gasthaus*, 1854.

He made his way round to the back, looking to climb. He was a free soloing mountain climber was the way he always thought about himself.

Now, he was trying to climb a fire escape ladder when someone pulled hard on his leg and he dropped down.

"What you doing up there, Mister little man?" Antony asked, holding an umbrella.

Moran made a menacing move and Antony showed him a fine looking blade he was never without ever since those unsolved murders.

"I'm waiting for a friend," Moran told him, backing away.

"Oh, my, you got a friend you need to reach up there on the fires escape? What your friend's name? And don't say Antony."

"He told me Antony could find him for me."

Antony sized up the little honkey. Something about him was familiar. Not the eyes. The eyes was wrong color wise and where they was looking wise.

"You looking for anybody with the name Williams? Six feet and then some tall man with a pale head and a look in in his eyes that ain't looking at anything?"

Moran jumped for joy.

"Yeah, that's him. I was supposed to meet him here."

Antony flicked the blade.

"That's some crazy shit you say."

"It's the truth," Moran said, raising one hand.

"Yeah, that's what the master said when he said three fifths is what that boy is."

Moran nodded.

"I get confused. That's why I'm out here."

Because Antony had earlier seen Williams walking around in the rain without a jacket or an umbrella and talking to himself, Antony now understood that what was going on here was in that spectre of things lining up weird that was absorbing minds lately in Founder like a door-to-door Jehovah Witless.

"He be in his room now unless he took to walking naked out here. Just follow me and put yourself right. This is The Founder and people live here got it all together. This place is older than shit so bend the knee brother, bend the knee. Understand me?"

"I do. I do. I'm bending."

"Your friend Williams. Different. Talks some heavy drinking man shit but he don't drink. You know Eve? His girlfriend he looking for?"

"Of course," Moran said, as they walked around to the main entrance. "Thy Fair Eve. Wonderful girl. Is she here too?"

Inside the lobby, Antony led him to the birdcage elevator.

"She's here and she ain't is what it is."

"It is what it is till it ain't," Moran said as they both got in the elevator and went rollicking up to Williams's floor.

Antony turned, stiletto back in hand.

"You a wise ass mudderfucker?"

"No, sir, I'm bending."

At the door Antony knocked.

"It's Antony, the all works man. I got your friend come to see you here. I'm to bed."

Williams opened the door a crack. He stared at Moran blankly.

"I leaves you two whatever you may be. I'm to bed."

"Sign the town hall red white and blue light petition," Antony hollered.

Sonny Bones' LamB came up the street and stopped alongside Antony.

Lucy Powell was driving.

"I need twenty for gas," she said to Antony who leaned his clipboard on the car and listened.

"I don't ask folks for money," Antony said. "Just to sign. It's a lot safer."

"That's cause you're crazy, Antony," Lucy said. "What's signing that gonna do for you?"

"There's so many things to be done and I'm just picking one," Antony replied. "Where'd you get LamB, girl?"

"It's a loaner from Sonny Bones. He went back to school in Texas."

"Oh, my! There's no kind of right schooling in Texas."

"Yeah, I guess. Never been there. Sun Bone is having some kind of big meeting at his hacienda. Tell me, you think I should drive up in this LamB on account of his son forgot to take it?"

"So, then you took it? I wash my hands on that, sister. Mister Chairman. I yield my time before this girl ruins my health."

With that he crossed the street and Lucy went pedal to metal and peeled out.

When they wheeled former Sheriff Jake Wilcox out of surgery and headed him toward intensive care Lucy Powell had been pacing the corridors of the County Mental Facility for almost seven hours. But even now they wouldn't let her see Jake.

"Just tell me why he's here," Lucy said, grabbing a nurse coming through the swing doors.

"Who's he, young lady?"

"Jake Wilcox. Former Sheriff. I heard he had a heart attack or something brain wise."

"That's hemorrhage or aneurism which is Neck Up and Neck up is us on this floor. Or, you need cardiology on the 3rd. You his daughter?"

"Baby sitter?" Lucy offered.

"That old man has babies?".

"If I get the mayor to say I should see him?"

"You're Harry Powell's daughter, right?"

The nurse, Evangelia Fata, asked, knowing full well that this was Lucy, the one the town couldn't tame. Or whatever it was they said about her at her father's café.

"Look, Lucy, if you go down to the second floor and give the nurse on duty there this note, you can have your dinner with a really nice bunch of people. I'll catch you up there regarding the sheriff."

"He's not the sheriff anymore," Lucy said, sadly. "He would never lock me up for minor stuff."

Evangelia scribbled something on a pad, ripped the sheet off and gave it to Lucy.

A young woman was playing a grand piano in the corner. It was like a restaurant because the tables were small and round and seated only four. But the diners were dressed down, in robes, most of them old, most of them women. Gentle vibes, wondering, but strangely laid back. A woman got up from a table in the far corner near the huge floor to ceiling windows and she waved to Lucy. Lucy walked over.

"I'm Mrs. Hearder," one of the old ladies said. "And this is Mrs. Woad."

"I know who you ladies are," Lucy told them. "When you were my teachers, you called me Looney."

"The name Looney is redundant in here, dear," Mrs. Woad whispered, looking around.

"Oh, yeah," Lucy said.

"Faye will take your order," Mrs. Woad said as Faye Fata came up to the table with a pad and a pencil in her hands. "Faye and my son Michael are sweethearts."

Lucy looked up at Faye who rolled her eyes.

"I'm everybody's sweetheart, Mrs. Woad," she said. "We've got meat loaf, mashed, carrots or broiled cod, stewed tomatoes and corn. Apple pie dessert."

"1965," Lucy said, remembering the fun she had the last time she was there.

"I have what I did in 1965 written out in my room," Mrs. Hearder said. "Month by month. Of course, some of the months are almost empty and a lot of what I did was the same month after month."

"After month after month," Mrs. Woad continued. "I know. All the same, the filler runs out and we miss it."

"I'll go with the meat loaf," Lucy said. "Oh, wait. Does that have meat in it?"

"Only if you want it, hon," Faye said.,

"What happened in 1965?" Lucy said to Mrs. Woad. "Did the Prozac withhold its miracle?"

"Coffee or tea?"

"Coffee. Black."

Faye jotted it down and said "Right back."

"I got somebody in here," Lucy said proudly, taking out a pack of Camels and lighting up.

"You can't smoke in here, dear," Mrs. Hearder told her. "It's a lung issue."

"Do you have someone in that pack of cigarettes that tells you things?" Mrs. Woad asked.

"No, not in this pack. But I've been out in the woods and down by the bog and I've heard things."

"What kind of things, dear?"

"I don't remember. I was with Mike Woad. He sleeps in the trees. In good weather."

"Darling, you're lively," Mrs. Woad said, taking hold of Lucy's hand and squeezing it. "Michael doesn't sleep in trees. You're mistaking him for his father. He slept in an old elm until he fell out."

'Is that how he died, dear?" Mrs. Hearder asked her friend.

"Oh, he died?"

Lucy pulled her hand way and flipped her lit cigarette on the floor.

"They won't let me see Sheriff Jake. And you can't say what you saw or heard because nobody wants to hear that. I'm sick and tired of everyone in this town not hearing or seeing what other people hear and want to say."

"Darling, what do you want to say?" Mrs. Hearder said gently, but Lucy just said she was hungry.

When the meatloaf came Lucy ate it in silence

Lucy was just finishing when Nurse Eve came into the dining room.

"I've got good news. That wasn't the sheriff they brought in. It was just a tourist who fell into the bog. Jake's fine. I called him and told him you thought he had a mini-stroke. He's on his way over."

Lucy got up.

She felt as if she had been made a fool of.

"I'm tired," she announced to them. "Nap time."

"But darling you didn't finish your meat loaf."

"I'll take it with me, Mother, " Lucy said, grabbing the bit of meat in her dish and stuffing it in the pocket of her sweatshirt.

She was gone no more than fifteen minutes when Jake walked in and began to tell the ladies about how he had been there for Lucy way back when and she probably never forgot.

"They called me to help bring her in when she got into some of her little escapades. One time she said to me 'Jake, I lost my support group. By coming back home I lost my support group.' I told her I'd help her find it and when I start looking in all the closets, bang! She slams the door on me and locks me in. Mayor Harry Powell told me to keep it a secret but I don't know about secrets. I mean I spent over sixteen years sheriff of this town pricking holes in the secrets. The law's gotta be against secrets. Like who perpetrated those couple a three weird crimes right on this property several years ago?"

"Lucy says she has secrets no one wants to hear," Mrs. Hearder told Jake.

"Secrets are sacred," Mrs. Woad said, shaking her head disapprovingly at Jake. "They're locked away for a reason. At some point in our lives we have to be locked out."

"You don't say?" Jake said, confused.

"Otherwise, the young, the very young would be overwhelmed," Mrs. Woad said very knowingly and without hesitation. "And the old wouldn't be able to go quietly into the sunset."

The woman playing Chopin, Jenny Woad, Woad's sister and Mrs. Woad's daughter, stopped and got up and left the room.

"You know Hank Bullard is in here," Mrs. Hearder said.

"You mean from Bullard's chickens?" Jake asked. "He must be over a hundred."

"They go deeper in here," Mrs. Woad said enigmatically. "More than a hundred. Very deep and far back. You remember things just being there in the room with them. They call it your object relations. I remember Aldo."

"Who was that, my dear?"

"Stuffed. He was stuffed. On my pillow."

"It's the flopping," Mrs. Hearder said, nodding. "It has something to do with the flopping. It releases the Orgone."

"I don't know about that but the nurses flop bodies every four hours," Mrs. Woad explained. "It's supposed to be for improved circulation and the prevention of bed sores but I think it's like turning an LP record over."

"Or moving the needle when it gets stuck," Mrs. Hearder added. "So they can think of something else. So they can go someplace else in their mind."

"And bits of their past memory shoot out into the room," Mrs. Woad said. "And you absorb them. Some of them are quite pleasant."

"It's nice to remember," Mrs. Hearder said. "And it prepares you."

"For what?" Jake said, nervous about ending ever since he lost his job. "I mean how?"

"To go further, darling," Mrs. Hearder told him.

"You can't stay here forever," Mrs. Woad told him.

"No, I can't," Jake said, excusing himself and getting out of there.

Outside the building it had grown very dark, either because of the time or an approaching storm or a dark cast of his mind but Jake wasn't sure. In the distance the spire on the town hall was aglow with a red, white and blue lighting and that was different. Every time he asked himself the question whether he would live long enough to solve those murders he told himself "Maybe, Jake. Just stay present."

It's not a classical physics trip to go down the road to where Sun Bone, the wealthiest and most powerful man in Founder, made John Williams and Dennis Moran members of his Executive Board. It's a quantum trip which I can't measure from outside the quantum world and it's of no use to try to put into words in a causal world of non-contradiction how this came about. It was yet another mystery invading Founder. Suffice it to say on this evening at the Bone mansion, a Queen Anne revival built in 1886 known among the locals as Gingerbread House, Dennis Moran and John Willams were at dinner with Sun Bone, Antony serving the multi-course repast.

"My ancestors built the railroad that led to this town," Sun told them. "The rails they hammered are just a few feet under the surface. The town was called New Wetlands then."

He paused and gave his guests an opportunity to digest his word.

"This horror will grow mild, this darkness light."

"That makes sense," Moran said, nodding agreement with Williams.

"What does?" Sun asked him.

He imagined that he owed his success in life to being able to think as other people did and then think better. So far, he hadn't been able to fathom how either of these two thought. And that he saw as a threat.

"Is there salt in this potage?" Moran asked Antony who was ladling the mushroom consommé in his plate.

"That's not relevant here," Sun said, annoyed.

"I don't know what Faye puts in the poor taj," Antony told Moran.

"Why are you here?" Williams asked Antony.

"I gets paid," Antony told him.

"He's a man of all work," Moran explained.

"You won't mind if I go into a little biography, will you?" Sun said, with a sweeping motion of one hand.

Over the fireplace was an eagle and on both sides glass cases of early Neanderthal monographed cufflinks, prominent brute skulls, mounted mayflies, leathery gonads, a deed of Trust, a prosthesis, and a ship's anchor. Along the walls were bookcases of quarter, half and full Moroccan bindings with gilt title on the spines.

"I enjoy lemon in my minestrone," Moran told them.

"This ain't no mini-stronsey," Antony told him. "This is straight up chicken noodles."

"Totally irrelevant, Antony. Get back to the kitchen."

A large globe of the world squatted like a sumo wrestler on a rich, faded Persian rug in the middle of the room.

Sun had probed all through appetizers and had come up with nothing. This troubled him since he knew he was skilled in reading the Occidental, small back water town mind. He began with his 14th century Ming dynasty ancestors.

"That was the beginning. But my real education came from people I came to know whose disordered minds held secrets that quite frankly made me, when cleverly exploited, into the zillionaire I am today. I seek the Black Swans."

"That makes sense," Moran told him. "Just what do you mean when you say everything is either won or lost at the grass roots level?"

Sun chuckled and went on.

"At the end of the day, I have peace of mind," Sun told them as Faye came in with a huge platter of spanakopita.

"Antony said he's non serve something for the rest of the evening," Faye said as she set the platter at the center of the table. 'So, it's me doing the best I can."

"There is nothing that has escaped Aphrodite," Williams solemnly told her.

Faye gave him a quizzical look. She had heard this guy talking shit at the café.

"*Non serviam,*' Moran said. "Antony will not serve the soup although he already has. There goes one Black Swan."

Sun gave Moran a withering look.

"I was saying," Mr. Moran, "that at the end of the day I have peace of mind. You agree with the importance of that Mr. Williams?"

"Man is a stream whose source is hidden. Our being is descending into us from we know not whence."

Silence followed that.

Moran lit a cigarette.

"Antony says this man Moran has a holstered pistol under his jacket," Faye said, cutting into the spinach pie, and cutting the silence.

"You are a spiritual man, Mr. Williams," Sun said nervously. "At least in so far as Occidentals can know the spirit in their materialist way. They let noise disturb silence."

"I use a silencer on this," Moran said, taking a Glock 19/30 semi-automatic from his shoulder holster and showing it to the table.

"These are the days of wine and roses," Williams said. "And good friends."

He raised his wine glass to Sun, who was staring at the Glock, stunned.

"Our interview is over, gentlemen," he said, pushing away from the table. "See to it that you don't shoot anyone, Moran. Williams, I'm going to support you for Mayor. You have a certain charisma that small town Occidentals appreciate."

"Where?" Williams asked, looking around.

All he saw was Faye, just staring at him.

"Here in Founder. You, sir, are a man of mystery. And mystery raises the common man above himself where he is glad to be. Or it confounds him into submission."

"Our brothers and sisters are the Angels," Williams responded. "But they are not mortal. We are. There is great mystery in that I think."

"He'll need the womens' vote too," Moran said.

"Faye, what do you think of Williams here as a mayoral candidate?" Sun asked.

She had not taken her eyes off Williams or the Glock.

"I think he comes across as just out of an asylum."

Sun laughed loudly. She was too weak to see what was going on.

"Oh, he's as mad as a hatter, alright. Same goes for Mr. Moran here."

"I abject," Moran said, winking at Faye.

"But you know, Faye, normal life is crippled with norms. Habits of the heart and mind and so on. The rules of the game. Then along comes a Black Swan and he remakes the game board because his mind is elsewhere."

"And that's good?" Faye said, wondering if she was the only sane one in the room. Antony was out in the kitchen eating the potage and he was short a full deck.

"Of course!" Sun shouted and Faye stepped back and eyed a knife on the table.

"That's how the world changes Faye. That's it."

His eyes were bulging and his face red going purple.

"That's it," Faye said. "I got it. Thank you, Mr. Bone, sir."

Antony popped back into the dining room.

"Excuse me, but I just don't want to be in any world run by that kind of madness coming out of these two sorry souls."

He hurried back to the kitchen.

Sun took a deep breath.

"True madness is rare but stupidity and ignorance fill the world."

"You're just a wise man, Mr. Sun," Moran told him, pouring himself some more wine. "Wisdom cries out from the kitchen but a wise man such as yourself sends it back into the kitchen."

"Don't try to suck up, Moran. You're a run of the mill sociopath. A clever madness is what you've got."

"You judge me harshly, sir," Moran said, "I …"

"Be quiet. You're useful to me. A useful sociopath is worth a dozen useful idiots."

"Poor Williams can't help it," Moran said, glancing fondly at Williams who seemed to have fallen into an eyes wide open coma.

"Don't you think he has a Jesus look, Faye?" Sun asked, studying Williams asleep.

"I wouldn't know. I make libations to the old gods. Old school."

Sun gave Faye a very displeased looked. Faye kept rubbing her hip

"You're dismissed, Faye. And tell Antony he will only be paid half time."

'That's the Jesus in you, right enough," Faye said, taking a tray of dishes out of the room.

"You know Williams here passed Baconey's SUIT test. He's not mad. Just broken hearted. Nobody knows what becomes of the broken hearted."

Sun glared at Moran. He couldn't seem to get one up on these two.

"Baconey? Dr. Baconey? The man's a clown. And what in God's name is the SUIT test.

"The four basic bodily fluids. Saltpeter, unguent, iodine and talcum. Williams is solid with all four."

Just then Williams woke up.

"And I applied my heart to know wisdom and to know madness and folly. I perceived that this also is but a striving after wind."

"Right there," Moran said, nodding supportively and pointing at Williams.

Whatever Williams said made Sun smile.

"Yes, right there. If he says that on the campaign trail, we can't lose."

"Golden," Moran agreed and then repeated his comment about the women vote.

"Ah! That requires an animal magnetism. Which I see in you, Moran. You will guide Williams's candidacy every step of the way in this regard."

"I'm your man," Moran told him, flipping his cigarette on the Persian. "Where do I bunk?"

"At *The Founder Gasthaus*. Campaign headquarters will be at *Sweeney's Right Now Café*. We will go right into mouth of the beast."

"*A dungeon horrible, on all sides round, as one great furnace, flamed; yet from those flames no light, but rather darkness visible serv'd only to discover sights of woe, regions of sorrow, doleful shades, where peace and rest can never dwell, hope never comes that comes to all; but torture without end.*"

Sun's lower jaw had dropped. He stared at Williams, the reciter.

"Milton's *Paradise Lost*," Moran told Sun. "Gold again. We can't lose."

Sun looked from one man to the other. Williams's recitation or Moran's knowing it stunned more. And they both knew someone named Milton. Astounding. Perhaps both were Black Swans. Black swans, the unrecognized startling outliers, the individuals whose words and actions overspill the ordinary norms and yet, if brought into the service of great enterprise can profoundly impact success.

"You are the surprise that escapes common observation," Sun now told Williams. "You are a game changer that remakes what little minds, those masses in the mud, believe is possible."

"That and he do smack of the asylum," Moran said, nodding. "About that there asylum. I got out by overspilling the ordinary norms they've got in there."

"What the hell does that mean, Moran?"

"I whacked Birke on the head and made a run for it."

Sun waved that inconvenience off. The price to be paid for a loyal sociopath.

"Birke? He's put his hat in the ring for mayor. Don't worry about him. We'll crush him.

Moran started to toy with the Glock once again.

"Put that away. I crush without the need of bullets. A caution, gentlemen. It's best not to say anything they can later pin on you. We shall water both sides of the street on every issue. Mystify and bury the rest. The essence of all good causes."

"Oh, Williams won't say anything anybody can pin on anything."

Mike Woad got out of the old pick up he had pulled out of the bog several years before. He counted and identified the vehicles already parked behind the asylum. He had found three bog eaten bodies in the old Ford and had slipped them back into the bog. The town didn't need any more reports of weird shit happening out in the bog and the forest primeval surround. He had seen on TV what a CSI team could do to a habitat.

The vehicles belonged to retired geezers, gentrifactors, survivalists, bankers, toe hold climbers, private predatory, Thoreau's great grandson old man Walt Walden Thoreau, and the usual town dregs, suspects. and cave dwellers.

When he got this medley around him, he told them what they could expect in the three weeks they would be in the woods, why they would be three weeks in the woods, and why, as the town's new mayor, he wanted them to return to native ways of the woods.

Former Mayor Harry wondered why Woad said he was the town's new mayor when he wasn't.

That question upset Woad.

"We're in the woods right now, right Harry? Am I correct?"

"Sort of the bog part," Harry admitted.

"Okay. Time moves differently here. It's not just the past that will pop up."

"Frank and I saw that," former Sherrif Jake Wilcox yelled out.

"It's the future, too," Woad continued. "I am attuned to all dimensions of time. Why you may ask? Because I've been open to not only what is here in the present but what once was and also what will be."

About three quarters of the assemblage shook their heads and went back to their vehicles wondering why they had in the first place responded to Woad's flyers posted all over town. But it wasn't the first time the Founder populace had run like a horde of lemmings off the cliff of their normal routines. The practice had become more frequent since a couple three bodies had been found murdered behind the asylum and no killer had been found. And Frank Coletti had never been right since he saw his dead father and his dead dog in the same locale. Beyond these occurrences there was the disequilibrium that everyone felt after certain individuals had been released from the asylum and allowed to mingle among normal, law-abiding citizens. In fact, one of the Louies, as the released lunatics were called, was running for Mayor.

"Do you know what I think?" Baconey said, an hour later when the seven of them stopped for their first rest.

He seemed unusually bothered with mosquitoes flying around him in thick squadrons.

They waited.

"Because I don't," Baconey said.

"I don't think Frank here is ready for things to open again like they did," Jake said, pointing to Frank Coletti who was seated on a log looking at his boots.

"Hey, where's Woad?" Antony said, looking around.

"He said he heard something back there," Earhart told them.

"I hear something back in there," Antony said. "I don't go back in there."

"He shouldn't gone back in there by himself," Jake said, pushing himself off the ground. "I better take a look see."

He ambled off into the brush.

"I hear Woad going through the garbage late at night," Lucy Powell whispered. "And then when I look, he's a raccoon."

"I thought you went back with the rest of them," Antony said, surprised to see Lucy right behind him.

"I did. I've learned how to be two places at the same time. Right now, I'm in my LamB."

That upset Antony.

"You ain't there, girl and you don't have a LamB, whatever that is."

"You're very quiet, Johnny," Earhart said to Williams as she walked over to him.

Instead of any kind of hiking gear and outfit he was wearing the same dark suit he always wore.

He turned to her. His face was pale, his eyes strange, not like his friend Moran's and very much less scary. More like Bela Lugosi.

"How can I live without thee," he said to her, "how forego thy sweet converse, and love so dearly joined, to live again in these wild woods forlorn? Should God create another Eve, and I another rib afford, yet loss of thee would never from my heart; no, no, I feel the link of nature draw me: flesh of flesh, bone of my bone thou art, and from thy state mine never shall be parted, bliss or woe."

He took her hand and she let him have it.

She thought it best to change the conversation.

"Do you think Woad is right? That there's something here that resents us?"

"Maybe the gods. We don't make libations to the gods anymore."

"No, we don't. But they were awfully silly those gods and goddesses, weren't they? Aphrodite arising from the foam of Uranus's testicles? Athena from Zeus's forehead? Of course, Artemis and Apollo were a normal offspring of Zeus. And so was Ares. Zeus again. A hopeless shameful philanderer. Really silly, no?"

"Zeus was the grandson of Heaven and Earth," Williams told her his eyes kicked up in brightness.

She wondered for the umpteenth time whether Baconey should have released this man from the asylum. Fascinating as he was.

"You better not announce you're a pagan if you want to be mayor," she told him, laughing. "They're mostly Christian here, some very odd and all disagreeing with each other, but the son they like is Jesus. No Zeus. Try to remember that."

"I do love the order of Spiritual Beings, "Williams corrected her. "The highest order the Seraphim, Cherubim, Thrones. Then in the middle: Dominions, Virtues, Powers. Lowest but angelic: Principalities, Archangels and then Angels."

"There's a lot of them, isn't there?"

"Before Angels there was magic. Before magic, there was Eve."

He stopped speaking and began to look around excitedly.

"I feel something has happened to the Woad Warrior."

"What? Hasn't he come back?"

They both rushed off in different directions to find Woad.

They had lost track of time. They sat around a fire that Woad had built. The fragrance of woodsmoke and Amanita was in the air. Tree frogs and bog fogs kept time to the crackling of the fire. Foxes screeched and rabbits cried. Eyes closed in sleep and then suddenly reopened as words were spoken in eerie tones. They would be different at daybreak and no one knew why.

Tents had been set up.

Evangelia began to tell them about not liking her job at *Founder Asylum* to which her cousin, Faye, told her she should try shifts at her father's café and Sun Bone's chateau.

"One of you or maybe both, one after the other, should marry Woad here and let him hunt and gather in the bog for you."

"I don't appreciate that, Earhart," Faye yawned.

Watching a wood fire send its crackles into the dark was hypnotizing.

"Antony is the real man of all jobs," Jake said.

"I don't appreciate that title, Jake," Antony told him. "

"I meant it in admiring way, Antony. I wish I had my old job back."

"The old ladies are the worst," Evangelia said.

"I don't appreciate the ageism in that," someone in the smoke said.

"Well, my mother will die and then life will be better for you, Evangelia."

"Wow! I wasn't talking about your mother, Earhart."

"I ran into a survivalist camp earlier," Woad said after a long while, whether to improve the campfire vibe or tell a truth.

"Some of your buddies?" Faye asked.

"No. Not mine. Not mine at all."

"Not interested in surviving, Mike?" former Mayor Harry asked, in good humor.

"I thought that's what you were doing out here," Faye asked.

"I'm a Thoreauvian"

"Oh my! Just what we need. More true words on what that poor man said two thousand years ago."

"Nature made me happy and good, and if I am otherwise, it is society's fault."

"Williams? You in that same denomination?"

"We had some of that sort back when I was sheriff. Somebody

was gonna blow up the town and there'd be no food or water. They had a stockpile of toilet paper and such."

"What did you do, Jake?" Earhart asked, knowing there was a story there and maybe one right now.

"Run'em in. Vagrancy. No gun permits. Reckless land use and such. Unsanitary conditions. That was about the time of them murders behind the Mental Institute. Now called just The Asylum."

"It's actually called *Sugar Maples Rest Home for Mind and Body*," Baconey said.

"Really?" Earhart asked. "Who told you that? Birke? You shouldn't believe anything he says. Didn't you tell me he failed your sanity test?"

"The SOOT," Baconey affirmed. 'Yes, he did. Twice. But he's the director. I can't commit him."

"Be that as it's gonna be despite what any of us think, what's with this new pack of survivalists, Woad?"

"Dressed up military, most Civil War, some pirates, Alamo types, Mexican Army & Navy Store outfits. A couple of Eddie Vaders, Davy Crotchits. Captain America and Billy. They thought I came out there to join them in their cause."

"Which is?" Earhart pushed. "Surviving after the apocalypse?"

"Oh my! The Jehovah Witless and the Seven Day Aversions and all them Lather the Saints and Pennycoastals are right out there camped in the bog?"

"Calm down, Antony. There's a story here and I need the facts. Woad, this is not an imminent Armageddon, is it? It's something else? Sounds like a mercenary encampment? They have guns?"

"I was asked what I thought about the government."

"That's it?"

"Did they use the word Copulation? Or Communism?"

"I didn't hear that. I told them I was running for mayor and they didn't like that. One guy dressed like the Lone Ranger said there was no room for a mayor and another guy in jackboots said the first thing that had to be done was line up all the mayors and shoot them down like dogs."

That testimony produced all the wailing of the Old Testament until they stopped that when they heard Woad laughing.

"I made all that up. They were just a couple of hunters hadn't had any luck so far."

""You're a shit head, Woad. I'd vote for Williams even rather than you."

"Sorry to hear that, Faye."

"Shut up. I'm out of this mosh pit in the morning."

"I'll go with you," everyone sang out but Woad.

When they were all asleep, he made his way like the woodsy Natty Bumppo to the militia camp that had so surprised him. He didn't care for those types in his woods. They worried the squirrels.

Because the eye is not satisfied with seeing nor the ear ever filled with hearing, what has been is what will be and what has been done is what will be done and there is nothing new under the sun. Except for what strives after the wind in Founder.

Deep into the Mayoral election, Michael Woad's rallies behind the Asylum are rocking flora and fauna with the uproar of Grateful Dead size crowds. Leonard Birke is hosting at the Asylum high energy, hypnotic techno Raves for which he's fast-tracking huge supplies of Ecstasy, Methamphetamine, Ketamine and Roofie, LSD and Heroin. "Heroin Chic" faces and bodies wandered around the Asylum at any time day or night so it is difficult to tell patients from Ravers.

"Birke's Promise: "Never Failing Supply Chain of Happiness!" platform runs neck and neck with Woad's mysterious "Everything Done Under the Sun, Below the Bog and in The Trees." What attracted Woad's followers was the idea of being in a safe place at the dawn of the New Millennium. Nature was like a bar of gold: it retained its worth regardless of the ups and downs of the "world out there." As Mayor, Woad promised to evacuate the town and bring all its citizens into a thriving bog and woods life in which all the magic of Nature's Spirit would fill them.

Frank Coletti ran on a "Bring the Paper Mill Back from Mexico" platform heavily supported by the 85% of the town that wanted their paper mill jobs back. Former Sheriff Jake Wilcox was Frank's best friend and biggest supporter. Somehow the jobs would come back if things just suddenly opened up at the right time in the bogs and woods out behind the Asylum where three unsolved murders had been perpetrated.

John Williams ran on what he called "Thy Fair Eve" platform whose meme was "The Founder Is a Woman" and which never became comprehensible to anyone but nonetheless riveted attention wherever Williams decided to speak, mostly *Sweeney's Right Now Café* and *Fata's Diner*. What was both comprehensible and incomprehensible to Rev. Goodnow was that Williams believed that Eve was a suitable Christian object of worship.

"This is more heretical and blasphemous than the Cadlick Virgin Mary idolatry," Rev. Goodnow boomed on the pulpit of the *Some Day Eventual Holiness Apocalypse Church.* "You hear this man who wants to be your mayor going on about the Lord God Almighty didn't give that sorry woman a perfect garden that she flung in his face to all our tragedy but when she got thrown out of there, she made a better world for us loaded as it is with weeping and wailing and sin and destruction. And so forth. That sorry, ungrateful creation out of a rib said she didn't know what living and loving was till she got thrown out of Paradise, perfect in every way as it was. Except for that snake that snuck in and sidled up to her and she went shopping for something Lord God Almighty told her was not for sale!"

What effect this had or anything had on Williams's electoral turnout or Birke's and Frank Coletti's turnout became harder to compute after Earhart Hearder threw her hat into the ring on a "I Can See and Hear the Dead All Around Us." As Mayor she would bring the town and the dead into alignment in the way the Sun, the Earth and the Moon are aligned in a straight line, the position is referred to as SYZYG, or when the Sun and Moon are in straight line, called Spring Tide.

The town was busy with all this trying to decide who might best fill what was really a position without any power over the affairs of Founder firstly because the town had been under Bank receivership since the days of J.P. Morgan and had lost any controlling autonomy, and secondly because half the citizenship were a masterless lot since founded by the legendary pirate of Nassau, Captain Flint and so each was self-willed and self-ruled. Under the skies of Heaven mind and heart are kept busy striving after wind until death ends such useless business. Occasionally, some in Founder thought about this and wondered why so much time was spent searching for wisdom or burning with passion, heart struck about whether it was part of a Celestial plan in which God, like an overwhelmed Nanny had given hearts and minds to keep busy with, or a rattle to a mewling baby, or a bone to a hectic pup. It didn't seem as if any of the numerous generations of experiences ever accumulated or kept to a point or were ever recalled from one generation to another.

"Nor will there be any remembrance of later things yet to be among those who come after."

For a time, it looked like things from the past were going to open up dramatically for the people of Founder but then nothing went off different than the dying breath of a loved one. You would think that heading toward the New Millennium as the town was everything would tighten up and fall into compartments of order the way a guest room is gotten ready for an expected guest. That didn't seem to happen. Sheets weren't changed.

The results of the mayoral election, meaningless as the Bank's representatives pointed out, went quantum in that what we were observing didn't turn out to be the case. A write in candidate won, namely Jenny Woad, Founder High School music teacher, won the election by four votes. A recount had been ordered and meanwhile the town was without a mayor. Jenny married and moved away before the final count.

Her cousin, Mike Woad, went back to his tree house; Leonard Birke was arrested by the DEA and scheduled for trial, represented by Klaus Birke, his Dad; Frank Coletti took to going on long camping trips with his son, F. Gregory, and with his buddy former sheriff Jake Wilcox. Frank was in hope of finding his dead Dad and his dead dog; Earhart Hearder went back to her job at the *Founder Chronicle* and announced that all the dead people she had been seeing and talking to were actually alive and living in town. Williams was a great disappointment to Son Bone who soon sold out all his holdings in Founder to a Private Predatory and moved back to Tulsa where he had been born. Williams turned to romancing Earhart, as he described it though she said he was stalking her and was considering hitting him with a restraining order.

She didn't because she was awfully attracted to him. Although talking to him was like riding downhill in heavy fog.

"People tell their lives into the landscape," Williams said as they both sat in a booth at *Sweeney's*.

She waited.

"And the landscape responds?" she volunteered, although as a good reporter she didn't like to put words into people's mouths.

"It responds?" he said, startled just as Glady's came over to take their order.

"I wonder if I can arrange an interview with Sweeney," Earhart asked Gladys.

"You could if you could find him. Actually, I don't think there ever was a Sweeney but I'm on my own around here in that opinion. Antony swears he goes out back and has a smoke with Sweeney every night?"

"Antony works here?" Earhart asked.

"Yeah, he gigs here," Gladys said and took her coffee pot to another booth.

"It's curious," Earhart said, taking out her notepad and writing. Some day she hoped to do a book about Founder. She'd call it A Fable.

"Yes, it is," Williams said, nodding.

She hesitated and then went with it.

"What is curious?"

"That if you look closely at what's around, lives unfold. The story of the dead who once walked among the trees is in the trees if you listen."

Okay, that wasn't what she was curious about. She needed to find the right channel here. He was sending on a far different channel than where she was receiving.

"You think Mike Woad is hip to that?" knowing she was asking if Willams thought Woad was as nutty as he was.

"It unfolds for everyone."

"Just exactly what do you mean by unfold? I need to be clear about this."

"It's a disclosure if you look through and not with the eye."

She thought about asking him the technique of doing that, but she decided she would just get a third something she didn't understand.She decided to jump tracks which in tough interviews she often needed to do. Tough was not a strong enough word here.

"Who's Eve?" I mean I know your mayoral spiel but who is she really to you?"

He shook his head; he broadcast upset.

"I know who she is. But where is she? I don't think she died. There's no mention of her death. I need to find her."

Okay. There it was. It didn't matter if Baconey said Williams passed his four point sanity test, because Williams was deranged on a more comprehensive scale like the way the S&P 500 Hundred Index told you a lot more than the Dow Jones Industrial Average.

Before she could shape a question that might lead to some enlightenment, Williams explained.

"You know the silken string of Ariadne that Theseus held so that it led him out of Daedalus' Labyrinth?"

"Kind of. Some of it. The string part."

"It led him to her. I am so tied to Eve and I feel the pulse of her in the pulse of the string and I'm led to her. "

With that he reached across the table and took both her hands in his. His eyes had the fierceness of the Minotaur's. She remembered the myth. Professor Campbell's Greek and Roman Mythology course Sophomore year at *Founder State*.

"To you," he whispered.

She was about to ask him if he was sure but she was so struck by knowing that he actually saw her, that for him she existed that she just reached out and brought his face close to hers and kissed him.

"Did you ever think the silken thread would wind up here"? she whispered.

"Here?" he stammered, falling back in his seat, shocked as if she had said Sweeney's was a good place for a marriage ceremony.

For of the wise as of the fool there is no enduring remembrance

"I heard Further is living in his car," Freddy said to Kenny as they rolled paint on walls in one of the new luxury condos owned by *Evolution Displacement*, a transnational with headquarters in Nashville.

"It's a thing," Kenny replied.

"We can bring him in if he wants to pick up the brush."

Kenny didn't like that idea.

"Dude didn't even show up at Mike Woad's Celebration of Life."

"I'd cut him some slack. He went off the high board when Abe died."

"You think so, bro? Was there any kind of memorial or whatever for Abe? Further and his sister Faye had him hauled off from the mortuary to the Crematorium. That's cold, bro, coming from his kids."

Freddy nodded.

"They didn't give him the kind of respect he thought he deserved. Further called his old man an old country Greek Patriarch. Abe willed everything he had to some relatives back in Greece. But Faye got disinherited way back when she started going with Mike Woad."

They both imagined that and laughed.

"Imagine if Cissy brought somebody like Woad in to meet you, bro."

"Yeah, but that ain't gonna happen. There's nobody like Woad."

"Yeah, and Woad took a tree dive. What was that all about?

Woad's slept in trees maybe 80 gazillion times and he falls and breaks his neck? Something fishy there. Jake would be all over it. You know. Another bit of strangeness in there."

"Yeah, well old Jake is being flopped at *Founder Restoration* so the only thing strange he might be thinking about is what the hell death is."

"Let me know if you figure that out, bro."

They were still rolling paint on walls when the owner showed up.

They saw her park her Porsche 718 Boxter.

"Nice wheels," Freddy said. "I wish I had gotten a chance to say which was better being rich or being poor."

Kenny laughed.

"Lady buys the brush we put in the paint we put on the walls and then bang we get paid and put that in the bank. Don't be a hater, bro. Lady married up. She was born here in Founder."

"Where'd the Up wind up?"

"He's reborn with a twenty something he left Lorna for."

"Judging by the car and this Italian Marvel she wasn't left broke. You get to know her a bit, bro? Lorna?"

"Just the standard schmooze the way Razpootey schmoozed Alexandra Federovnyvich."

"We painting her place next?"

"It looks lovely, gentlemen," Lorna said at the doorway gazing at the walls.

"It does have a look," Kenny said, stepping back to admire. "You were right, Lorna, about the Double Shade Eggshell. Freddy and I were going with Off White. We're getting the hang of these Italian Marvels."

"Italian marvels?"

"That's what Kenny calls these Nouveau Chateaus going up all over now. They put in Italian Marble in kitchens and bathrooms. We were dry wall painters pasted wall paper in the old days."

"We're not used to world travelled cultivated owners like yourself, Lorna. Freddie and me have to expand our vision."

"Don't lie to me and tell me I have a natural eye for interior design," she said, laughing. "My taste was developed here in Founder and you know what that is. My ex never missed a chance to tell me I had Contadina taste."

"What's that?" Freddy asked.

"It's Italian for a peasant. We've vacationed in Tuscany a few times and now he thinks he's Count Bolla."

"Wow! Count Bolla! Goofy. Sounds like it's good he's Ex'd out of your life."

"I wish. It lingers. I have this deep need to get back at him. Somebody will need to stop him. He'll go through a dozen naif nubiles, suck the life out of them and then discard them."

She paused.

"You don't look to me like the life was sucked out of you," Kenny told her. "When did you live in Founder?"

"We left about at the time when everyone was talking up those murders out behind the Asylum. Did they ever solve them?"

"No. But former Sheriff Jake Wilcox is still looking for clues."

"Oh, I remember him! Huge bear like man with a gruff voice? And thank you, Kenny. I'm in my mid-forties. I have no illusions about escaping my past."

"You know we might have been at *Founder High* around the same time," Kenny said. "You recall, Freddy?"

Freddy shook his head.

"But I recall you two," Lorna said. "You were the Prom King weren't you Kenny?"

"Damn, that's right. I was."

"Lorna Neelye. My father owned the target range at the edge of the woods not far from the bog."

Freddy and Kenny shared a eureka moment.

"He was shot and died on that range," Lorna said, in a hushed voice. "It was ruled an accident but Jake Wilcox said my father wasn't shot at range level but elevated angle from somewhere in the woods."

"I don't ever remember that coming up," Kenny said.

"Me neither."

"Jake Wilcox was voted out of the job," Lorna told them. "And what he found never went anywhere."

They could hear the paint drying.

"My mother packed us up and we left town right after the funeral."

"Comprendo," Freddy said.

"So, if I may ask," Kenny asked, "why did you want to come back."

She was not far from tears but now she tried a laugh.

"I don't know. PTS? Divorce does that to you. But I think it's something else. But I don't know what. Probably never will. But I'm here. Some part of me wanted me here."

"You got a loose end," Kenny said nodding.

"What?" Lorna exclaimed. "Is that like a loose nut in my head."

"Kenny means your father dying like that is a loose end you want to or need to deal with."

She was clearly absorbing the new info.

"I'm a mess," she said, wiping at her eyes.

"You might want to talk to Dr. Baconey," Freddy told her. "He patented the SUIT test to figure out what's inside folks eating them up they don't know anything about."

"He talks them into …"

"Submission?" Lorna said and the three of them laughed.

"Anyway, why go to him? I should just talk to you two. My consiglieri house painters."

"Eve thinks I talk too much."

"Your wife?"

Kenny just didn't respond.

"Hey Michelangelo, we better get back to it before the paint dries," Freddy said breaking the silence.

"High praise," Lorna said, but she was looking curiously at Kenny.

"He painted the Cistern Chapel lying on his back," Freddy told her, but the mood had changed and after a few more words Lorna left.

"Call if anything."

Both nodded. They watched her getting into her Porsche.

"She's something, bro," Freddy remarked.

"Divorcé with a purse. We're gonna need a lot more Italian Marvels. Cissy's tuition at Yale is knocking like John Bonham on drums."

"What's Cissy studying again?"

"Wealth management. She's been interning for Goldfish Jacks."

"Cool."

"You know that son of a bitch ungrateful bastard Frankie Junior won't lift a finger to help that poor son of a bitch his own father?"

A Caregiver passing by where Lucy Powell was seated by former Sheriff Jake Wilcox's bed tapped Lucy's shoulder.

"Lower your voice, Lucy. You're upsetting the clents."

"What the fuck!" Lucy shouted. "What are you a bed pan cop? And who the fuck are the clients? These are a bunch of sorry ass mother fuckers on their last legs. Except Jake here. He never put me in jail."

She reached out and patted Jake's hand.

"You mean F. Gregory?" Jake croaked.

"Yeah, fucking F. Gregory. You know I went to the Prom with that fuckwit?"

"I'll have to call a Restorative Guardian, Lucy if you can't restrain yourself."

"Go ahead. Make sure you tell him I've got a gun and can put a bullet up his ass. Just go away. I'm talking to somebody I love who's in his last hour. Can you deal with that?"

When the Caregiver had walked away, Lucy told Jake that she didn't really think he was in his last hour but still she had some bad news for him.

"Woad fell out of a tree and broke his head back behind this place?"

"No. Yeah, well he did, the stupid son of a bitch. It was rumored. Maybe fake news. That was a year or so ago. You know he was my hero growing up. I remember when he was running for mayor."

"Who is the mayor now? I lost track."

"Some prick. I don't know. He's been here a minute. Look, what I have to tell you is that they found Frank's body out there where the bog seeps into the woods."

That news got Jake's head off his pillows.

"Was he murdered?"

"Well, they say he didn't fall out of a tree. Coroner calls it foul play."

"That fits in," Jake exclaimed excitedly. "That fits in! I got to get out there and pick up the clues before the rain washes them out."

Lucy thought about telling him that he couldn't go out there because he hadn't walked in six months or more and it didn't look like he was ever going to get out of that bed until they shoveled him into that new shiny Crematorium built right on the south edge of the bog.

That thought fired her up.

"That goddamn *Founder Crematorium*. Built right on the spot where Rev. Goodnow's *Somoan Adventure Holiness Apocrafull Church* was before they creatively destroyed it. You know I think that cantankerous man of God Goodnow would be screaming all the way into those fires as the Crematorium's first customer."

"Who built it?" Jake croaked.

"Private Predators and fuckwit gentrifiers!" she screamed. "I'd shove that lot into the fucking Crematorium in a heartbeat."

"You have to calm down, lady."

Lucy looked up at a guy of the type she called beef.

"I'm grieving here" Lucy told him. "This is the way I grieve."

"Best to grieve privately, Miss so you don't disturb "

"Why the fuck are their private military in here?!" Lucy screamed. "What is this? Kabul?"

She was on her feet now.

"Oh, my, don't you ever give this poor man some peace."

It was Antony, coming up to her fast.

"I just told him about Frank," she explained, pointing to Jake who looked at both of them from behind heavily drugged eyelids.

"You need to tell her to show some respect or I'll take her out of here."

"It's all good, Robert E," Antony told the Restorative Guardian. "I got her meds right here."

"Okay," Robert E said, and giving Lucy a last warning look, walked away.

"That don't look like the Robert E. you pointed out the other day."

"I calls them all Robert E."

"Yeah," Lucy said. "Whatever."

She was looking at Jake.

"I didn't want to give him bad news."

"There's a whole box of tissues there for you girl. Anyhow, that's old news. My Influencer already sent me that word. I say you don't want anybody to murder you, stay out of that bog."

"Is that what that twelve year old told you?"

That was another lot, Lucy thought, the Influencers, she'd rush to the new Crematorium. Them, the Stakeholders, the Gentrifiers and the Meritcrapacy. And the No Responders.

"She's got sixty thousand Robert E. followers and none of them speak English and this Influencer only speaks English."

"Good for her. Give me your phone. I need to call F. Gregory and tell him what a fuckwit he is."

"I'm sure he waiting for that call," Antony said, giving her his phone.

"This wasn't near a bed pan, was it?"

Jake started to moan and Lucy went over to his drip and worked the valve.

"You gonna kill that poor man, ain't you?"

"Stop playing Uncle Remus, Antony, and help me calm Jake

down. He needs a bit more of whatever this is."

"Morphine drip. This place is on the watch for inheriting relatives fooling around with the drip."

"Well, I ain't one of those. Jake doesn't have a dime. The city cut off his pension the year Jenny Woad didn't get elected. Bitch didn't even show up for her own cousin's Celebration of Life service. She got the call and just said he ain't dead. He ain't the type. Couldn't take time out for her own brother's celebration fest."

"More ticks than people at that one."

"Jenny was my piano teacher. We played chopsticks together."

"I remember. You been playing keys with the Ramakrishnas is what I heard."

"They wanted a younger face in the band as a draw. I'm not that good."

"And your face is not exactly that young."

"Go back to being Uncle Remus."

Jake had ceased moaning.

"Is he dead? You might have over-dripped him. Gotta go."

"Wait. Is that you doing that 3AM radio show? You talk some shit for sure."

"Well, that ain't me then."

"Yes, it is. I've heard your Oxbridge voice. It's you. I fall asleep listening. I just wanted to thank you."

"He do the voices," Antony whispered in her ear. "The Dark Reverend comes on right after."

"What? Right after? I'm long gone by then. Besides Further's battery dies out."

"Oh, my, you sleeping in that fool's van too?"

"I was out in the trees before Woad dropped. Who's the Dark Reverend?"

"Rev. Goodnow."

"I thought he was cremated?"

"Dust don't turn to dust anymore like it used to," Antony said. "I need to move along. There's a luncheon at noon with the Centre Ville Pied a Terre Club followed by a Happy Dividends Hour I can't miss."

When Lucy turned, one of the Caregivers was flopping Jake on his back with all the gentleness of Two Ton Tony Galento body slamming Haystacks Calhoun.

That night as Lucy stretched out on the lower level of Further's van parked out back of the *Founder Asylum*, she listened to Antony's broadcast, *Gnostic*, swimming wearily in the wonderful Oxbridge accents used, for goofy reasons, Kenny had told her.

"Former Sheriff Jake Wilcox has volunteered to personally sweep the Asylum bog in search of clues leading to the murder of Frank Wilcox in line with his thirty-seven year search of clues leading to the arrest of one or more who perpetrated the crimes of murder in the same locale. At present, former Sheriff Wilcox is in ICU at *Founder Asylum* and is not expected to live.

Arrivals to Founder in the last ten years may be unaware of the Bog Mystique which involves the opening of certain curtains of the present into the ancient past of the bog, a past in which the remains of The Founder may be found, although bones that have come to the surface have not been conclusive in this matter.

A pilgrimage Camino de Santiago de Compost style with full luxury tour packages is expected if authentic bones do surface.

Sheriff Wilcox will be aided in his search this time out by F. Gregory Coletti, multi-million dollar financier speculator on the movement of prices, and Michael Woad, who fell to his death last year but has been sighted in the same woods and bog area he lived in before he fell and broke his neck.

Members of the *Centre Ville Pied a Terre Club* will serve sandwiches at the *Founder High School* privatization launch on May 1 from noon till 2, where Headmaster Dennis Moran spoke these words: "As Headmaster of the Clinic I would like to welcome you to this building. dedicated to our students' rehabilitation. Each inmate I can assure you will be incentivized to maximize initiative toward innovation and growth. We don't agree with locking up young minds in money making drug therapy schemes or false narratives and conspiracies you hear in this town on every street corner but prefer to break through all that bullshit with Open Carry. This Glock for instance."

Mr. Moran had engaged in a shootout with the Sheriff's department some ten years ago when he blocked *Global Community Private Predatory* from entering the *Nouveau Chateau Estates* previously owned by Sun Bone but bought by *GCPP* in a deal that many players in that game called slimy. Mr. Moran did thirty days in *Founder's Asylum* where he had previously been an inmate, which perhaps explains his approach to *Founder High School* as a Bedlam for Boys, although the high school is co-ed.

Mr. Sun Bone retired to his home town in Tulsa, Oklahoma where his great wealth was allegedly swindled by his Wealth Manager, whom Sun's son, Sonny Bone, now living in a vintage LamB parked in different locales in town, called one of his father's goddamn "Black Swans."

Sonny Bone, his inheritance gone, has returned to Founder and now lives mostly in his car in the bog vicinity.

Subsequent to the High School launch, Mr. Moran hoisted a few at *Sweeney's Right Now Café*, expressing his dislike of being part of a Happy Hour among Dividend Recipients who could kiss his ass.

The DR's Happy Hour is at seven each evening at the new *Shangri-La Club and Spa* erected on what was previously sacred town bog. Club membership is required, such requirements now challenged by Chapter 6 of the Employment and Equal Opportunities Services by the *Bedtime in Parked Cars Association*.

I hope to tell my dear listener how Moran was appointed the new school's director. Wait. I am mixed up in my notes. Dennis Moran was not made the *Founder High School Director*. Mr. Klaus Birke was appointed and if my notes are true, though unbelievable, Moran brained Klaus Birke with the butt of his Glock and then forced his way on stage to make his speech.

To the lovely Lucy Powell whom I hope is listening, Get out of Further's car.

Good night to all my old Founders. We were there at the beginning. We are accessory to the end. The voice of deceased Rev. Goodnow is on the air now."

"Goddamn, Mudder humping Black Swans!" Sonny yelled from a corner booth at *Sweeney's*.

"Look, Sonny, I'm here for the whole story, not for a tantrum."

Sonny had an I'm sorry face as he looked at Earhart.

"I'm sorry, E. But you know when I think …."

"Don't think. Just focus on what I'm asking. Why did Sun unload everything and skip town?"

Sonny shook his head back and forth the way you do when you can't see night from day.

"Did he need to liquidate all his holding for some emergency?"

"Yeah, probably. Maybe. What emergency? Wait, maybe he knew I was going to be kicked out of Phoenix U. I failed all my courses. I got in with a bad crowd."

He paused and looked sheepishly at Earhart. She, for her part, knew this was going to be a tough interview. Sonny never ever answered a question in any way that you could point to it as an answer. This would be hard to get across in a two column piece. But she had to get something. Why Sun Bone, the guy who the whole town thought would lead them into the New Millennium, sells everything and ghosts all of them was a question on every old Founder's mind for the past ten years. She needed the story. She needed the job. The *Founder Courier* was a print daily whose circulation went down every month. The online "journalists" were beating them into oblivion. And all they did was shoot out what no newspaper in the past two hundred years would put in print. They didn't print. They just typed rant and bullshit and hit send. And then the like-minded gathered to them. Humans were bottom feeders. Made her look at Sonny, the once and future scion now living in his car.

Sonny was mumbling something about his girlfriend.

"What did she have to do with any of this?"

"Maybe I got kicked out because of her. I think I had the kind of girlfriend that didn't like it if I studied. So, I didn't study. Except sometimes. But not enough. You think?"

"She didn't want you to study? That sounds like bullshit. If you tell me she didn't want you to drink, dope or gamble. But study?"

He grinned.

"Maybe my Dad found out she left me."

"Now, please focus. Why would he care about that? He cashed in multi millions in properties because your girlfriend dropped you?"

"Maybe. Could be. His mind was very Far Eastern. Oriental for sure. Maybe."

"Inscrutable? Right? Like Charlie Chan. Come off that line, Sonny, Sun Bone was not anything Asian. Near, Far or middle."

"Oh, wow!" Sonny exclaimed. "That is very nasty for sure. Why would you say that?"

"Because I read it on his passport. He was born in London. Sunderland Bone. Caucasian and Brit to his bone."

Sonny just nodded.

"You knew that, didn't you."

"He had puffy eyelids. He thought being Asian and looking like he was seeing through you was better in making deals. Maybe. My Dad thought that if you were silent people would talk more and they would reveal more than he would. Maybe. He was sharp."

She hated to bring it up.

"So why did he get into all that Black Swan crap? I mean as sharp as he was, he wound up trusting a guy that cleaned him out. Sent every dime your father had to a zillion off shore untraceable accounts."

Sonny leaned forward and it looked like he was going to kiss the table. He beckoned her with one finger to get her head close.

"I think the Black Swan is here," he whispered.

She sat back up.

"Everything ok, here?" Gladys asked, coming over to them.

"Fine," Earhart said as Sonny jumped up.

"I got to move the LamB or they'll tow it."

He hurried out of the café.

Gladys took his spot.

"Sad what happened to him," Earhart said. "Living in his car."

Gladys didn't seem sympathetic to Sonny's plight but she didn't follow up on it.

"It's a thing now," Gladys said. "Living in your car. Or somebody else's like Lucy Powell is. Harry did all he could for her but she's on that spectral part, whatever that is."

"Further works here, doesn't he?"

Gladys frowned.

"I pay him enough so he doesn't have to live in his car. He likes it."

"I'm sure you do. It's funny how Abe and Sunny Bone wound up disasters."

"Well, they're dead," Gladys said sharply, which was her default style. "Disasters don't reach them now. One would hope. But I'm not bent in that line. Dead is dead."

"He sold the café to that coffee chain?" the reporter in Earhart probed but Gladys was prickly at even the most gentle probing.

"My business here didn't force him to do a stupid thing like that. He did that himself. Faye and Further should have been brought in but no, that lot had to rehearse every goddamn father and sibling drama the world has ever seen. Now the son is living in his car and the daughter is cleaning houses of people who own. Period."

Gladys moved to get up. Earhart put out a hand.

"So, can I ask you a reporter question?"

"Isn't that what you've been doing? Okay. Go ahead. Just don't make up the answers. Every dumb son of a bitch comes in here thinks that's having a conversation."

"There was never a Sweeney? It was always you?"

Earhart expect a blow up but it didn't come. She had touched a warm spot.

"There was a Sweeney. We were supposed to be married. Liberation of Kuwait. His body got liberated from his soul. He had to get in there and fight. Women keep the species going. Men gotta fight."

She pulled a pack out and lit a cigarette below a No Smoking Sign. She saw Earhart look at it.

"Maybe the Daughters of Massacred Iroquois will come in and arrest me for smoking. They've got a chapter here now. They think The Founder came over on the Mayflower. Or before. Anyway, Sweeney, wanted to fight but it was for Kuwait that he didn't even know where the fuck it was. And then after I heard all the Kuwaiti with Italian marble homes and house slaves went off to Paris while Sweeney was protecting their way of life. I get sick thinking about it."

"And the café?"

"He wanted to go to culinary school. He didn't. I did. I got a loan from Sun Bone and started this place."

"Interesting. What do you think happened to Sun? I know he liquidated, took off and now he's dead. But what do you think was going on with him that triggered all that?"

Gladys gave Earhart the look she was known for- a cross between fuck off and go fuck yourself.

"I don't know. I was square with Sun money wise way before he left but whatever happened to him started here in Founder. He was old school smart but what's swept in here he wasn't prepared for. You know what they say about con artists and thieves? We're into a whole new level of that shit and Sun thought he knew the game when he didn't know shit. His son could have helped him but between you and me that Sonny is an idiot and always was. He would have blown through any inheritance if there had been one and wound up living in a car anyway. That's my two cents. Can I get you something?"

Earhart shook her head and thanked Gladys for talking to her.

"Just don't print anything I've said or I'll sue your ass."

She smiled and walked away.

For to the one who pleases him God has given wisdom and knowledge and joy, but to the sinner he has given the business of gathering and collecting, only to give to one who pleases God.
Ecclesiastes 2:26

Brothers and sisters, I have gathered my flock and collected their sins which wear my soul to shreds and I have tried to collect enough money to keep this tabernacle heated, lit and welcoming.

I am a sinner then? Is everything I've done to be given to those who please God? Where did their wisdom come from, these chosen, if they never worked hard each day but each day only get wiser in knowing there's no fairness in the world, a world which these sinners didn't make but they're made to live in it.

I am not a preacher who set out to please God but one who gives the same amount of respect he gives to all of us. I don't see much of that respect and now that I'm dead I'm still not seeing it.

But what do I see? What reason would you have to love your neighbor, to love someone you don't respect? Why would you do it? I'll tell you. You don't. You can't love him as yourself because you believe you're better than he is. He ain't you. Flat out what it is. But he's got what you don't have. It don't make any sense. He's got the sports cars, the Italian Marble mansion, the trophy wife. Why the hell is not coveting your neighbor's wife one of the Commandments? It says his house but it's his wife that pulls you in., like Eve pulled in Adam. That dance was written before there was a word at the beginning.

Go Big or go home. That's not a Beatitude. What you do unto others is what's left over after you do unto yourself.

There are nine levels of Angels and how many in each level we don't know but you can deduce that however many there were they didn't cut the mustard so the Almighty God needed another creation. Us humans. We're not Celestial spirits like the Angels. We're Beasts.

"With regard to the children of man God is testing them that they may see that they themselves are beasts. For what happens to the children of man and what happens to the beasts is the same; as one dies, so dies the other. They have all the same breath, and man has no advantage over the beasts, for all is vanity. All go to one place. All are from the dust, and to dust all return."

And the Angels fell apart and the rebels were sent to rule in Hell. There's a drawing board failure in construction there. Twice repeated. For we Beasts, we don't start out as Beasts. I don't know what Adam and Eve were in the proper digs assigned and how long they were there, enjoying without knowing what enjoying was, but they did disobey, got evicted, and so the only world we know is born. There's the Genesis. Lower in degree from Angels but of kind the same.

Face it, Eden was never a place we were designed to fit in. From the get-go, I see that. But I'm dead. The Almighty saw it before it happened. Free will is like a long road ahead to a blind man. There was nothing to will or not will, to will to win or will to lose, to will to sin or will to obey. Nothing when the choices don't' exist.

And they didn't exist for Eve. Adam? He was uxorious. He chose Eve over the Almighty. That was the disobedience, an amazing disrespect of the Almighty whom, as the Bible shows, never got over it. Eve didn't bring death into the world. The Almighty did. She kept on living. Sassy but not Almighty.

I preached God's Will whether shit happened or the lottery was won. Obviously, the Almighty could be extracted from the equation as unconnected, not germane, neither here nor there. If the hand of the Almighty is in all things, good and bad, we're talking about Don Corleone. We are striving after wind and all toil good and bad is for the wind whether we bring the Almighty into the game or not.

I'm done. I may be back or some Fallen Angel may show up to drag my ass to wherever. Sleeping in the Void or sunk in the Abyss. But most likely waiting for a judgment. I've already judged myself blind when I was alive."

"I should never have won that scholarship," F. Gregory moaned, sitting by former Sheriff Jake Wilcox's bed at *Founder Restoration's Sunset* brand new addition.

He had first been directed to ICU but there he was told that Jake had been re-assigned to the Sunset Wing because, as was explained, Jake's condition had stabilized.

"It's our full palliative wing."

"So, he's still dying?" F. Gregory had asked.

"We're making him comfortable," was the sharp response. "We don't focus on dying. We meet death with a plan."

Now, as he looked at Jake lying there, eye lids fluttering, drugged to the comfort level, F. Gregory remembered this man well over six feet tall and two and a quarter hundred pounds at least, tears came to his eyes. It was like the sap from a great sugar maple had drained out and left a kind of ragged mound of flesh.

They don't focus on dying? Well, it damn well will hit them in the face, others and their own.

He surmised that was why he preferred numbers to words and the stupid thoughts people put into words. There was never an equation solved with words. His success hadn't come from any string of words that built dream worlds or confounding beliefs and ideologies swept away and forgotten by a new breed of thinkers and artists. He had made a breakthrough at the age of 19 concerning curved three dimensional space applied certainly to all dimensions. His work on invariants had been the foundation of seven different competing versions of string theory. All of his mathematics revealed what was deeply surprising, exciting and for him personally exciting.

He realized he was telling this to Jake who seemed to be in a more wakeful state now that F. Gregory had arranged for a temporary drug moratorium. Pain couldn't be quantified. On the scale of 1 to 10 what would you say your pain level is? F. Gregory laughed. When you're drugged to a vegetative state it's like cancelling out the troublesome part of an equation so you can pretend you solved it.

"Tell me if the pain is too much, Jake. But you want to be more on the side of awareness than drugged out. The pain is the only way to get back, Jake."

F. Gregory realized he didn't know what he was saying. This man, who was never disappointed in him, who understood somehow that Frankie Jr. was different somehow This man. He loved him. If he could go camping with his Dad and Jake. When he did. His cell was vibrating. He ignored it.

"Lucy…"

"What Jake? Hey, it's me. Frankie, Jr."

"She…she opened the drip," Jake said. "They caught her."

He pointed to something that wasn't there.

"Tried to get me out of here," Jake croaked a laugh and then coughed.

"Lucy Powell?"

Jake nodded.

"Sleeps in a car. You should find her."

He remembered Lucy. He had taken her to the high school prom where she had made a scene. Not a good one. She had a flask of whiskey. They both got drunk. But she did a strip. He didn't. She got ejected. He hadn't seen her after that.

"What happened to my father, Jake?"

"We gotta go out there and find him."

"What I was told was that he was murdered. Is that true? Why would anybody murder my Dad?"

Jake tried to raise himself up and Frankie, Jr went over and helped him.

"I was about a foot away from needing reading glasses and that would explain things. Suddenly opening up. We were in the woods but this wasn't the woods behind anybody's house. You go up north past the town, which is already north of Sameold Bay, and you go back in town. Time, I mean, you go back in time and then you go back to town. I went along with Frank and little Frankie because we had a couple of open murder cases on the books and in some ways the fellow that Frank had seen -- you know, in that bit of scene changing Frank spoke of -- fit, more or less, the descriptions we had of a fellow hanging around town the day of the murders, April 23rd, bodies found out behind the *Founder Asylum*. And I'm the sheriff. I mean I was the sheriff back then."

This all came out in a rush as if it was pouring out of some place deep where it had been.

And it had been there also for F. Gregory. Things now opening up to what had been. Cataclysmic things like a murder. Another dimension of time so overwrought that it could remain there but like an appendix bursting had to burst through. F. Gregory felt he had the mathematic of that. But he needed to be there. He told Jake that. Jake shook his head.

"Lucy told me they're going to clear cut the woods and drain the bog."

"What? "

"I went out there last night," Jake began, "and I saw Mike Woad doing what I was doing."

F. Gregory had heard of Woad's fatal accident. The woodsy hero of his youth.

"What were you doing out there?"

That question visibly confused Jake. His hands fluttered and then he winced in pain.

If he could take a little more pain, his mind would grow clearer. That was a thought, like all thinking in F. Gregor's view, that didn't

equate. A mind that could clearly voice what was true on one side
and on the other side former Sheriff Jake Wilcox dying painfully. It
didn't equate.

He called for a nurse and when she came over, he told her Jake
was not comfortable and that in fact he was drowning now in a deep
pool of pain. And he, F. Gregory, didn't have the mathematics to
solve that. But he could go into the woods to see his father. He knew
he would be there. His time would push open into F. Gregory's.
Frankie, Jr's. Out of a misty dream, a path would open. He
wondered what and who was behind destroying those sacred
places? Everyone in Founder knew it was where The Founder came
from and where The Founder still was.

He also had a desire to see Lucy Powell again. In widely different
ways, they had been alike. Alike in that they were different.
Inequalities.

Earhart was busy at her laptop writing her article when Williams
came in the one door to the outside they had. You got to it by the
stairs on the side of the *Sweeney Café*. It was a noisy place up above
the café but Williams seemed to like it. He hadn't minded the dorm
he was in at the Asylum. She found since they had begun to live
together that indeed home was where the heart was and her heart
was with Williams. In turn, she wasn't quite sure if he was devoted
to her or his mystical sweetheart, Eve. Sometimes it seemed that he
thought she was Eve come right out of those gates over vast
millennia to him. And sometimes she thought she just reminded
him of Eve. That was alright if that's all she was going to get from
him. But then there were times that she knew that he knew it was
her. That she wasn't mythical/visionary but a real person, one who
might have obeyed the Almighty and not messed with that apple
tree, one who would have stomped that snake into the ground.

The most rebel in her was in her reporting. And if one of the same
sort who were buying up the town bought the *Founder Chronicle*,
she'd be given the boot. But she didn't worry about that. Bottom
line was she could sleep in a car like half the town was as long as
Williams was with her.

It was that kind of feeling that fired up her temper, causing her
to go after Williams as a dominating male whose talents and smarts
didn't measure up to hers. And he wasn't that at all. He had

something more annoying. He had some deal going with a damn numinosity as explained to her by Baconey. By definition, Baconey told her, a sense of the numinous was all about something holy that was hidden and couldn't be grasped rationally but nonetheless enfolded a person in what wasn't in the world but transcended it. Williams had that. If that wasn't enough Williams conflated any idea of the holy transcendent, a Celestial presence and realm, into the figure of his sweetheart, one person, one woman somehow the Eve of Genesis and at the same time a presence inherited by all the daughters of Eve.

"So, he's more of a kind of pagan than Christian or anything like that?" Earhart had asked Baconey.

She knew answering these questions about Williams wasn't easy for Baconey because there was a time when it looked like she would marry him. And have a normal life, maybe some financial security. Eddie Baconey wasn't bad but she never really got over that he had been given the name Oedipus. And other stuff really frightening. And then she allowed whatever it was that emanated from Williams to detour her from a normal life. Nothing was emanating from Eddie Baconey.

"I'd say he's drawn to this sweetheart the way most of the gods were drawn to Aphrodite. Does he make libations to her?"

"Who? Aphrodite? He's fond of an old beech on the perimeter of the bog and the woods. He pours out some water at its base and has this screwy look on his face."

"Total pagan. But harmless. Don't forget you're his Eve. Adam forsook the Almighty for Eve."

And now as Johnny came in and came over and kissed her on the cheek, she kind of wondered if the kiss was a kind of offering to Eve. Or maybe Aphrodite. Williams knew more about the Greek gods than the medieval monks knew. They had to really know who the enemy of faith was.

"What are those?" she asked as he sat down at the small kitchen table, which was also the dining room table and also where stuff was just thrown, and he thumbed through a small notebook.

"Notes I took at the first meeting of the new Town Council. I'm the recording Secretary. I'm not supposed to talk. Just write the minutes. Write the minutes?"

She could see that thought had taken him somewhere.

"Might I ask who gave you that job?"

"Do you think I can't do it?" he asked, as if that thought came to his mind.

"No. You can. But you have to pay close attention and record what's going on. You have to admit you're not a close observer of…of anything."

She wanted to say that he spent most of his time observing what wasn't there and the rest of the time in a kind of Taoist trance. Not good habits for a recording secretary.

"How do the new Council members seem to you?"

She might as well get an article out of this. She should have been invited as a member of the Press but she wasn't. She didn't know there was a meeting. Skepticism was the primary tool of the investigative journalist. Why was the daft but lovable Johnny Williams recording secretary and why wasn't the *Chronicle* invited? It was things like this that irked her. She should take up a faraway look and talk admiringly about Adam.

Williams began to read from his notes. What she heard right off was something filtered through a mind always thinking about something else. The totally unreliable recorder.

"Baconey was late. A patient went bananas in his office. He said a sedative injection did the trick.

Baconey was always to be called Dr. Baconey.

He said his first name is Oedipus."

"Really? He told everyone?" Earhart interrupted, taking notes on her laptop. This was too good not to publish.

Antony Ethiopian Nicodemus said exsqueeze me but who made Bunny the Lord of the Manor House"

Earhart couldn't help laughing.

"Who's Bunny?"

"Council member. He was called that back at Yale because his last name was Wabbit.

"Gladys Farquarson made a point of information motion and she said she was a woman.

Bunny apologized for addressing everyone as gentlemen.

Gladys said her name should have been Farquardaughter.

Billly said: Oedipus? Isn't that the guy who killed his father and married his mother?"

Dr. Baconey said: Unintentionally. Thus, the tragedy."

"Who's Billy?"

Williams looked up from his notes.

"No one knew. Antony said, who the bejeesus is Billy. Billy took out a pair of pistols at one point and put them on the library table.

Then Gladys said how do we have a gangster as member of this Council"

"You were meeting at the Public Library?" Earhart asked.

"There was a motion to rename the Public Library the Private Membership Only Resource Center."

"Got it. What else?"

"Some old wrinkled man said his name was Founder and he said he was The Founder of *Founder*.

Bunny said that J.P. here is a descendant of The Founder and will bring this town to the attention of the Titans"

"I take it J.P, is the old wrinkled guy?" Earhart asked, typing furiously.

"Slim Jimmy then called for a vote on the proposals."

"And who is Slim Jimmy?"

"He seemed to be a lost young man."

"Did someone say that at the meeting, Johnny?"

"No, it was what I felt."

"Okay. Go on with your notes."

"Antony asked Mr. Slim Jimmy if he was trying to pass as a black man?

Slim Jimmy said his Nonna was an Octaroon.

Billy said that Slim Jimmy could put *Founder* on the GPS of a 15 to 20 year old demographic.

Gladys Farquarson said that none of what Billy said is any good and she moved to eject Mr. Slim Jimmy right out the door. She said she was still waiting on who the fuck the Titans were.

Harry Powell woke up and shouted who the hell are the Titans?

Then Billy said Let me tell you, Miss Farquat whatever your name is and this old geezer that your asses should be off this Council for not knowing who the Titans are. Right here at the table you are sitting next to a Titan of Finance, a Titan of Rap Industry, myself a Titan of Crypto Tech and J.P. there, a descendant of the pioneer founder and owner of this town. He's a Titan of Real Estate Investment, Development and Foreclosure. And every Titan is heavily positioned in AI and robotics.

Gladys Farquarson said they could all fuck off.

JP then said he was not here to claim ownership although his company *Global Community Private Predatory* . . ."

"You're kidding? Did you get that right? You've done an amazing job, Johnny but that's his company's name?"

"It has ownership of *Founder Asylum* as well as *Founder Prestigious Pre-Kindergarten Prep* and the renamed library now open to club membership at a yearly rate.

Gladys objected to the firearms on the table pointing at her.

Antony said oh, my and he didn't think he was going to stay for more of this.

Bunny said he was sorry to see Mr. Ethiopian go as he was our diversity member.

Then JP moved that we drain the bog and clear cut the forest.

Gladys Farquharson said that they couldn't do that because God only knows what all is back there and in there.

Bunny asked the Council not to forget the bog iron that God knew about.

Gladys Farquharson said there's history, our people's bones, magic and mystery and the soul of this town back there. People who actually have lived here longer than a minute choose to be sunk in that bog.

Bunny was shocked by that and asked who had been sunk?

Gladys Farquarson mentioned Ethel Hearder and Betsy Woad had been bog sunk as they requested.

Billy said that dropping a couple of old bags in the bog wasn't going to stop progress and that the bog iron would be sucked out and shipped to China

Then someone said that calling two senior citizens of Founder a couple of old bags was an insult that offended the cosmos and the cosmos was a great Avenger."

"I take it that someone was you, Johnny?"

Williams nodded.

"What did the member with the guns say?"

"Billy pointed a gun at me and said "Bang!"

Earhart sighed deeply.

"Oh, Johnny, there are so many ways you get me to worry about you."

"You shouldn't worry about me, Eve. I'm no longer the Recording Secretary."

She felt like smacking him across the head and at the same time swaddling him like he was her baby. None of that was good she felt, shivering. Since she had gotten to know him, or enough of him for her to think she knew him, she saw that he was always about to go down that driveway in time and space that led back to a padded cell at *Founder Asylum*. Now it could be behind bars in prison.

"You've got more notes?"

She had already given up getting any kind of sense out of the notes, at least any coherence for a *Courier* article.

He nodded and went on.

"Gladys Farquarson said there are clues in the bog. We just

haven't been able to find them.

Harry Powell mentioned the three murders never solved back there.

Someone said that sometimes what is long gone is only not seen because time has taken us elsewhere. But there are places in which time is befuddled. It doesn't know it's not the past. And in these places, what is past, sometimes long past, and dead comes up right next to us and we see that in these places there was never death. I found that in the bog. It's what The Founder found. I saw him briefly."

Earhart stopped typing.

"That was you again, wasn't it, Johnny?"

"I'm not supposed to talk.

Billy said "How did this guy get on the Council?"

Harry Powell said that back in the old days the town always had a preserve the mystery member and John Williams was elected for that spot. The tradition went way back to the Nebraska/Kansas Territory twitch trials.

Williams put down his notepad.

"Then I was asked to leave and the Council was to consider the Recording Secretary position vacant. Gladys repeated herself and said all these new members should go fuck themselves and she told Billy everyone in the town had a gun and knew how to fire bullets into meat.

Williams got up and went over to the sink and ran the cold water.

"Not a job for you, is it Johnny?" she said rubbing his shoulder.

He turned and looked at her.

"If you don't find the place where things don't change, your life is like a ship caught on a lee shore."

"I guess," she said, trying to visualize that.

"It's unseasonable cold," Klaus Birke said, throwing some brush on a fire which immediately flared up and shot sparks into the darkness.

"Don't throw that last year's Christmasy tree stuff on it," Moran told him, stretched out on a wool blanket across from where Klaus was lying on an inflatable, fire in between them.

"We better get some logs to get through the night."

"Yeah, go get them Klaus."

"I'm way past getting up. What time is it? Once I'm down, I'm down. Cold like this I'm not rising to take a piss."

"Well, just don't piss the fire out," Moran said, reaching out for a burning faggot to light his cigarette.

"My head still hurts where you beamed me back there at the high school."

"My apologies. I should have just shot you."

"You know we could be sleeping at the high school. I still got the keys they gave me."

"They'd pick you up put you back where you belong."

"My son, that jackass, ran that place into the ground."

"I'd say the opposite. He got everybody high all the time. Baconey got you released, didn't he?"

Klaus laughed the way you think a nasty snake would laugh if it could laugh.

"You hit my son over the head, didn't you? How did you get away with that?"

"Same reason he wanted you out of there. It's easier on him if we're gone. Guy like you, Klaus, is a pain in society's ass and putting you in a cell don't really make you any less of a pain. The proper way to deal with a pain in the ass like you, which is my way, is to erase you, the way a heavy dose of morphine erases pain. Extermination. Not incarceration. That's my platform. You need to be cleansed."

Klaus muttered some expletives angrily.

"Besides, you're older than dirt," Moran told him. "You need extermination. First thing tomorrow, I'll fling you into the bog."

"I'm gonna shoot you in the face while you're sleeping," Klaus growled.

"Whatever," Moran said and the two of them closed their eyes and listened to the fire crackling and the Fossil Forest cretaceous fauna.

"I once broke out of a Federal Prison like your son is in now," Moran said, about thirty minutes later and colder.

"Was it warm cause all I can think about now is getting warm. Old bones don't generate any heat."

"You know I could sleep in any warm bed in those luxury Italian Marble condos they're building."

"You talk big, Moran."

"This is about the time you catch sight of the Woad Warrior moving around."

"I bet he had some pretty fine tree sleeping arrangements back in there. He knew how to generate heat eighty feet off the ground."

Moran had taken his Glock from his pack close by and laid it across his chest.

"You hear something?" Klaus asked. "I'm not used to bogs and woods. I went to Yale."

"Sometimes I think all this here likes me," Moran said, "And then sometimes I'm afraid that I'm just prey lying here like this."

"I heard on that late night limey radio that Sonny Bone's looking for the perpetrators of his father's financial fall and his untimely death."

Moran didn't reply

"Weren't you Old Man Sun's bodyguard or something?"

"He was going to make me mayor. He thought Williams was the Black Swan to beat all but Williams was more nuts than me so I'd be mayor."

"Son of a bitch. Told you that to your face? My own son, that supply chain degenerate moron, told Dr. Baconey, that wimp in diapers, to give me that SHIT psychopath test. Nobody passes that and so it was a set up."

"The SOOT? I passed it. Self: I strive to be a person who others love and admire; Other people: I need the help of other people to do so; Objects: I share with others whatever objects I have; Time-Life is short and I hope I can leave my fellow humans better than when I came in."

"You said all that? But they didn't release you? You laid too much bullshit on them. You're a get out of my way fuck you all guy."

"Baconey said I was a high IQ sociopath whose intelligence had led me to realize that the reverse of the Bible's Beatitudes treated me best. That's a perversion of a normal psyche Baconey told me which brought in the psychopath part of my head. All of which made me a lifer in a nut house without parole. If I was to get out, I might upset the social apple cart. Very likely could attain a high office of power."

"Or wind up sleeping in the woods freezing your ass off."

Moran let that go by.

"You know why, Baconey asks me, you can't keep chimps in the home when they adult? Because by that time they figure they can kick your ass and punch your lights out. They learn we're weaklings compared to them. They got enough brain power to evaluate their experiences with humans."

"You think Sonny Bone is going to come looking for you?"

"Probably. Among others," Moran surmised. "But I'm not too worried. I guess Sonny Bone is living in his car so I don't think he's going to be able to come looking for anybody until he gets food and shelter sorted out. Besides, that boy has an easily befuddled brain. He's not even sure of his own name. He thinks he's Accidental."

The fire went out though the two mentioned a few times about the need to get up and look for wood.

"You know Frank Coletti is somewhere close by dying," Klaus whispered to himself. "You think his murderer is running loose in here?"

"Yeah, there's been murderers running loose in here for hundreds of years. And bodies. The bog has a bottom with them stretched out."

"I think I'm going find a car to sleep in tomorrow," Klaus said, shivering.

"That's a plan," Moran agreed. "Me? I'm going straight to *Sweeney's* for a full Irish breakfast."

"She's Irish, is she"

"Gladys? She is what she says she is and you better not disagree. Gladys would have eaten every apple in that garden and spit the pits out. I tried some game on her time ago. Didn't go over."

"Figured you was a high I.Q. sociopath psychopath?"

"I guess."

They both laughed.

"Lovely ladies. Creative. The womb of the world Williams says."

"I heard him talk over at *Sweeney's*. He's something else, ain't he?"

"For sure. But what? I trust him on women though. Eve puts a smile on his face. Thy Fair Eve is how he talks about Earhart. I guess he knows her name isn't Eve but maybe not. He's a hard one to figure."

"I think they'll get a net on him some time soon. I heard he was in some gun play at a Town Council meeting."

"We shall escape those nets, Klaus, you old bastard. But Eve? Ah, yes, Thy Fair Faye. Daughter of Eve."

"How come you're talking like you're Irish?"

"I do the voices, my friend. I've got me a world of voices up in here."

He tapped his temple but Klaus couldn't see it as it was too dark.

"You know I think I was the only sane one in that place. My son wanted me dead that's why he put me in there."

"Is that a fact?" Moran said, breezily. "I'd like to see Faye again.

She's cleaning houses now I hear for the at home lap topper young couples heavily invested in war materiel is what I hear."

"Right now, I feel as sane as a priest. Freezing my nuts off but sane. Can you throw a log on that fire, bejeezus?"

"It's out. Keep the inner fires going, brother. Keep them going. And shut up. I need my sleep."

"Right there proves something. Inner fires? That the sociopath part of the psychopath one?"

"Dying is what's calling you, brother."

"I wonder if she has apple pie?"

"Gladys? Probably."

"I still don't understand what you do," Lucy Powell said to Frankie, Jr, as they sat in the Rolls-Royce Phantom Frankie had come into town with. "Or why you're so filthy rich?"

"I run an investment fund," he told her.

"And?"

"I look for hidden patterns in price movements. We make tens of thousands of small bets and we come out ahead 51% of the time."

"And that's enough? I mean to own a car like this?"

"It's leased," he said, hoping that would make him less filthy rich in her eyes. He regretted not returning to Founder in a moderate price sedan. And he should have left the chauffeur back in the city.

At that moment, the chauffeur tapped on the window. He had a large bag in hand.

"Oh, is that our picnic lunch!" Lucy exclaimed as the door was opened and the bag handed to Frankie. The chauffeur pressed some buttons and a small table top appeared.

Lucy pulled out a couple of wrapped sandwiches.

"Chicken Parm," she said, happily. "What did you get?"

"Liverwurst red onion."

"Whew? It sounds awful. Is that a thing with your crowd?"

Frankie watched the way she chomped into her sub and it took him back to high school days trailing after her.

"I don't have a crowd," he said, unwrapping his own sandwich.

"Oh, that sounds so sad!" she exclaimed.

"I'm not sad," he told her, thinking that now that she brought it up, he wasn't gay and he wasn't happy. He was just kind of neutral, like a prime number.

"There's a couple of Cokes in here," he told her.

"I can't," she said, her mouth full. "I'm in CA. Cokes Anonymous. I drink Matcha only now."

"I'll tell Daniel to get you a bottle."

"No, silly. I don't drink that."

She pulled out a can of coke, opened it and swilled. It seemed to make her happy.

"Okay, now that you've enticed me to your Rolls and fed me royally, what's this all about, Frankie? Or should I call you F. Gregory. You know your father hated that name."

"Yes, I know. My stepfather gave it to me. He said I couldn't get into Yale as Frankie."

"Oh, he was a dick. I'm sorry. I shouldn't have said that."

"He wasn't a bad guy. Just different. Different from my Dad and Jake. I didn't go to Yale. I went to MIT. Mathematics. That's how I got a scholarship. I think in numbers when others think in words."

"I try not to think," Lucy told him, reaching into the sack for another chicken parm. "I'm different too. They told my Grandpa Harry that I was on the spectrum. I think in colors and signage and leaves falling and wafts of wind and ..."

She stopped and burst out laughing.

"Look how seriously you're looking at me. I can think. Don't worry."

She made him smile. She was lovely. How had he forgotten this?

"You know about numbers?"

"Yes, F. Gregor!" she said, mockingly.

"Frank. Frankie. Please."

"Ok. Frankie. What about numbers?"

"I don't really think about them either. I mean it's something different than thinking. I can't explain."

"I can. It's the immediate pre-reflective, pre-predicative apprehension of what the rational mind cannot grasp."

That caught him just about to take a bite.

"Wow!"

He remembered how in class Lucy would suddenly pop out with stuff that amazed the whole class.

"You know we're a lot alike," she told him, seriously. "Your stepfather and your bio Dad are dead and my Dad died when I was three."

Frankie put his sandwich down.

"Jake says my father was murdered."

"Oh, Jake told me that your father is lying out there in the woods and he's alive."

"He told me that too."

They sat silently and then Lucy said

"So why aren't you out there looking for him? Jake would but Jake is four feet from dying."

The question upset Frankie and he both knew and didn't know why.

"I've been thinking about that."

"But?"

"The woods," he said in a low voice.

She put a hand on his arm.

"Yeah, let's get out of this regal wagon and walk a bit."

They walked in silence for a long while, finding themselves at the cusp of the Asylum and the woods beyond. She headed for a path that took them into those woods. He hesitated.

"Memories?" she asked, looking back at him. "Or, afraid to find your Dad somehow in those woods, breathing and waiting for you?"

"That wouldn't make any sense. They found him dead with a couple of bullets in him. I paid for his burial. I'm here to do a Memorial of Life. Jake knows that."

He felt himself shaking.

"Look, Jake's been convinced that there were people murdered in those woods and those cases were never solved. He was the Sheriff then. He didn't solve them. It all haunts him. He's been not right. I mean I love Jake but I'm not going to validate his delusions by going in those woods searching for a man who I know is dead and buried."

"It's exactly what I would do," Lucy said, defiantly. "And I'd expect you to do it also. I know we'll find him."

There she was. The Lucy who could never be made to touch ground.

"I said I ran an investment fund. That's a practice, an offshoot of what I am. I could be a poker player or a pollster or a meteorologist. Hundreds of things. But at bedrock, I'm a mathematician. And though there are imaginary numbers in advanced calculus all the relevant phenomena in the world that you and I are in are described by using nothing but real numbers. I'm in no way prepared to jump out of the real world."

"I find that very, very sad, Frankie. Actually, that's the F. Gregory in you. And I don't like him."

She was indeed an unsolvable equation.

"Look, don't you expect to see Mike Woad in those woods also? Am I right? And he's dead too."

"I've seen him. Williams has."

Frankie laughed.

"Williams? When did they let him out? He's been seeing some phantom nobody else can see. Of course, he'll see Mike Woad. He expects to see the dead but he can't see his own face in a mirror. He lives in an imaginary world."

"Well, he goes out looking for your father which is what you should be doing."

Before he could say anything, she set off on the trail into the woods. He watched her go.

This hadn't turned out as he had expected. It wasn't just that he feared finding the impossible, his father lying in there, dying but not dead, but that whatever would create such a situation would take him, absorb him, push him into seeing what couldn't be. He didn't want to be that 12 year old in those woods watching his father become his grandfather, seeing something of the long past imprinted somehow in those woods, a scene of violence, an observation made in one time frame intruding into his own. He didn't want the present he knew to give way like a curtain in a wind and take him to where he had no words to describe, leave him laughable to all as Jake and his Dad had become after countless retelling of their fantastic experience in those woods. And worst of all, he didn't want to enter a reality that numbers could not solve.

It was only later that night as he lay in his bed at *The Founder* that he saw a portal. Quantum mechanics was an exception in reconciling the real with the imaginary. There were underlying quantum states and governing equations involving imaginary numbers that could represent the real. He tossed and turned thinking that it was Schrodinger's box that was the woods and bog out there. And his Dad was the cat inside, both dead and alive, beyond any calculation of certainty.

The next morning, he left a note for Lucy at *Sweeney's*, spoke to the Eden Bower Funeral Director, giving him instructions that former Sheriff Jake Wilcox was not to be cremated but the body dealt with as Lucy Powell wished.

"Lucy probably wants me to lay him out in the woods or sink him in the bog," the Director told him in his funereal voice.

"I don't want to know about that," F. Gregory snapped. "It doesn't matter. I will pay your highest fee. Regardless. Do whatever Lucy Powell wants."

On the drive back to New York, F. Gregory concluded that leaving was the best thing to do. He had too big a hunch that this town of Founder was somehow a multiverse microcosm and if he stayed he would never find the mathematics to get him out.

But he would miss Lucy. Reckless and fun. Explosively radical and impossibly stubborn. There was no mathematics for her either.

Dr. Oedipus Baconey had never been in a Federal prison to visit anyone nor did he feel he would ever be an inmate. He found out soon enough that Leonard Birke was in a private correctional institute run by *Global Community Private Predatory*. He had to go on the Dark Web to find that out.

Birke wasn't surprised to see him although he admitted that Baconey was his first visitor in the seven years he had been incarcerated.

"I figured you would wake up one morning and say "I should visit Leonard. It's the moral thing to do. I'll do it."

Baconey didn't know what to say. Birke had a way of making him seem a fool and that he, Birke was pulling his strings.

"Took seven years for you to do the decent thing and come here for a visit. What did you bring me?"

"They took the pie I was bringing from *Sweeney's*."

"Did you have a file in it?"

He laughed.

"I brought some books and magazines"

"Last man standing reading books and magazines. I got my own laptop for porn searches."

"They're really lenient in here?" Baconey asked looking around Birke's accommodation which was something like a suite at the *Founder*.

"If you pay them," Birke sneered. "And I got the money. Boy, do I have the money."

"Raoul!" he yelled and there was a knock and an inmate came in.

"Bring us a couple of cold ones, Raoul."

"You got it, jefe."

"Is …is he …"

"Raoul? Yeah. Armed robbery. He robbed a bodega with a water pistol. Maximum life. He had his cousin Raoul defend him."

"Seems kind of harsh."

Birke laughed. He had a bad laugh, Baconey thought. A bad laugh was an inappropriate laugh. It revealed sociopathic tendencies.

"Everybody in here gets to stay. Think of it like a hotel that likes to keep its paying guests."

"You could appeal?

"You implying I got all my drug supply chain loot so I should be able to hire Percy Macy? That would happen if the Cartel wanted me out and they don't."

"The Cartel?"

"That was my supply chain management supply. They think I stiffed them. Yeah, I did. It's in the genes. Got it from Klaus. You know the story. The scorpion. Or is it a snake? Anyway, you help them out and then they bite you as a thank you saying it's in their nature."

Raoul came in with the beers, nodded and left.

"He keeps an eye on me for the Cartel. They'll probably put a tail on you now."

"Me? Why?"

They seem to think I've got a stash somewhere that belongs to them. You might be my contact guy."

The beer bottle almost fell out of Baconey's hand.

Birke laughed again.

"Calm down. I was just gaslighting you. I got a top law firm working on getting me out."

"So, the Cartel…"

"I think they always show up in the movies, right?"

Birke was giving him a once over and it made Baconey nervous.

"You know why I hired you and not that magician, Tristus?"

"You said you preferred science to magic?"

"I don't. Give me magic anytime. You think you begin in some place of reason? We come out of nowhere, pass through a subway tunnel they call life, and then shuffle off to nowhere. That's magic, Baconey. Dark beginning. Dark end. It's all fucking magical mystery tour."

He did the laugh again, more sinister Baconey thought.

"It's a farcical condition, Baconey. Science wants respect. But nothing, nothing at all merits it. I hired you as a front. You were the only one in that psychiatric hospital that made us look like we weren't what we were, an old time lunatic asylum cum drug dispensary You and a couple of others got us past the Fed's GAO. Everybody else was in on the drug supply chain."

"I didn't lean on psychopharmacology."

"That was perfect. We weren't just dealing and pushing drugs to the outside. We were using respected bullshit talking cures. But the main reason I hired you was to get Klaus the fuck out of the place and out of my hair. I needed the paperwork with your signature. And I knew he could pass your lunacy test. He did, didn't he?"

Baconey nodded. Birke's father had sailed through. He was as sane as the Pope.

"You know why he passed? I coached him."

"Who put him in there in the first place?"

"That was Sheriff Wilcox. He brought Klaus in for interrogation over a couple three murders in the woods out behind our playhouse. Wilcox couldn't figure the old man out and brought the State's mental examiner in and he certified the old man as full looney."

"Did Klaus…"

"Have anything to do with those murders? Well, let's put it this way, he wouldn't have had to have a reason."

The laugh again.

"I have to tell you, I was nervous around that guy. My Dad. He thought I was the one keeping him in there. You don't want to get him pissed off at you. By the way, Oedipus. You killed your Dad, didn't you? Just kidding. Where's Klaus now?"

"I heard over at *Sweeney's* that he and Moran were forming some militia rebel group out in the Fossil Woods."

"Moran? And my old man? That's a pair."

"Why did you let Moran out? I knew he was faking my test. He's that clever."

"I didn't let him out," Birke said angrily. "He escaped and he was too much trouble to go after. I mean after Sun Bone took him up as a body guard. That was dumb but old Bone was dumb. Sold himself on thinking the fucked up could make him billions."

"The Black Swans."

"Yeah. The minds out of the box. But thing is they all belonged in the box. Including the ones he turned his financial operations over to."

"It's sad. His son, Sonny, is living in his LamB."

"Yeah, well he was straight dumb. Sun thought he had a hold on the magic."

"You know he wasn't any part Asian."

"I knew that. Part of his game, I guess. You know what's at the heart of all that Oriental jabber? The Tao and so on. Mystery. Don't try to figure it out. Just go with it. Like go deaf and dumb to living and then when you die you join the Great Nothingness."

"I think there's a lot more to it than that," Baconey said.

"The light of the Sun and the loveliness of ladies," Birke said loudly. "That's what gives us life. I'm into both."

"I guess visitor time is over," Baconey said, getting up.

"In here? Sit down. I've got to tell you something."

Baconey sat back down.

"First, as I was just saying. The ladies. Get yourself a special lady. You going to need one."

Baconey pondered that. For a while, he thought Earhart liked him and something would come of it but Williams drew her to him, to his whatever.

"Okay. Just saying. But Tristus has given me a glimpse of what's coming."

"The Magician? Magistus?"

"He's in here. A lifer. Not playing with a full deck but not dangerous. He sees a dark battle coming between time was and time going to happen."

Baconey waited but Birke made it clear that that was it. He didn't see the specific need for a woman in that prediction but he didn't ask.

"Was he any more specific?" Baconey asked.

"Founder," Birke muttered, angrily. "The woods. The bog. The town. Visit's over. Get lost."

Kenny was doing some clean up in one of the seven bedrooms at Lorna's Italian Marvel when he heard the car. When he looked out the window. It was Lorna. She came up while he was tamping paint can lids down.

"It's after 7," she said, coming in the bedroom. "When do you stop working?"

"Freddy took off. I'm just prepping for tomorrow."

She walked around the room.

"How many of these are there? Bedrooms?"

"Seven"

"Oh, my God! What was I thinking? I've only got one bed."

"They don't have to be bedrooms."

"No, of course. But, I mean, what could they be?"

"I think most people would have an idea."

"Your laughing at me. Divorcé with full PTS. Truth is when I saw the amount of the settlement . . ."

She paused.

"He had sold his whatever software startup to Bill Fates the year before. There was no pre-nup. I mean he had nothing but an algorithm when we married and he never thought about ever having money. He's got a cyberspace head not a Wall Street one."

"So, you got half?"

"We were both in shock. He didn't challenge it. I got a wealth manager. And…and a therapist. And this seven bedroom house."

She laughed.

"No longer. The therapist. I got better advice from my grandma. She was born and raised here in Founder. Sally Trotter?"

"Sure. Freddy and I got one of our first paint gigs painting for Mrs. Trotter."

"Look, how would it be if I took you to dinner? I'm starving. Unless you've got dinner waiting at home."

"No. Cissy lives on campus. State. No dinner waiting but …"

"Consider it a business meeting," Lorna said. "I need advice on what to do with seven bedrooms. Actually what to do with this whole….What do you and your brother call it?"

"An Italian Marvel on account of all the gentrifiers coming in to town showing us photos of these Italian villas in magazines. Goofy."

"Well, on the advice of my wealth manager, I should immediately buy real estate. Tax advantage and I'm building wealth. So, I rushed into this."

"Yeah, the *Nouveau Estates* was Sun Bone's project. I think some investment group owns it now."

"You don't like it? Ostentatious, right? Luxury living isn't the Founder I remember."

"No, it's not but after the paper mill closed, living any which way is hard. So, I got no problems with it."

"The owners don't rankle you?"

She was smiling.

"Well, some are a bit much. But you're from here, right?"

"But I'm now filthy rich. That's a horrible club I'm now in."

He sighed.

"I'll take you up on that dinner, if you cease and desist being goofy."

Lorna was at a back table in *Sweeney's* when Kenny, freshly showered and hair tied back came in. Gladys was at the counter, pencil in hand, reading glasses on. She looked up and nodded when she saw him. They were good friends. He was one of the only ones in town who knew the Sweeney story.

"You clean up nice," Lorna said, as he came over to her table. "You definitely fit a style."

"I do?" he asked, sitting down. "You've got your own."

"Tell me. Divorcé, rich, mid-life crisis under therapy probably drinks too much and doesn't know she can't go home again."

"I was just thinking about your voice."

"My voice?"

"Do you sing? There's a good tone to your voice. I bet you can match a pitch."

It was Faye who came up to them to take their order.

"I bet she can," she said. "Hey, Kenny."

"Hey, Faye. Lorna meet Faye. She's new in town. We're painting her place."

"They're the best," Faye said.

"I didn't know you were working here."

"Yeah, it's in my blood. Diners. Meatloaf and chili. They call to me."

"Special for me," Kenny said.

"What's a special?" Lorna asked.

"Meatloaf, mashed, green beans."

"I'll have whatever kind of large salad you have."

"Ok. No surprises. Welcome to our homey little town, Lorna," Faye said and went to another booth.

"She seems angry. I'd say a Joan Crawford part."

"Well, her old man didn't leave Faye or her brother a dime. Cut them off."

"Whereas I got cut in with multi millions."

"That much? I'll need to review our bill."

"So, the first thing that strikes you is my voice?"

"No, now it's the money. Freddy and me started out in music. We still play some gigs around town."

"I kind of figured there was a hipster behind the paint can."

"Hipster?"

"Here listen to this" She fiddled with her phone and then read out loud:

"The late James Dean, for one, was a hipster hero; it is tempting to describe the hipster in psychiatric terms as infantile, but the style of his infantilism is a sign of the times, he does not try to enforce his will on others, Napoleon-fashion, but contents himself with a magical omnipotence never disproved because never tested. As the only extreme nonconformist of his generation, he exercises a powerful if underground appeal for conformists, through newspaper accounts of his delinquencies, his structureless jazz, and his emotive grunt words."

"Wikipedia," she told him, putting the phone down.

"Magical omnipotence? That's goofy. I'll tell Freddy. He probably didn't know."

Two hours later they were at the bar. She was drinking *Side Cars* and he was drinking *Guiness.* They had been calling each other goofy for a while and laughing.

"Not of This Earth," Lorna said, pointing to a black and white framed movie photo. "1957. An alien comes to Earth looking like a human being so he can get blood to save his planet."

"Now that's goofy. The film, and you knowing it. What about that one?"

He pointed to another photo.

"Day of Wrath," Lorna said, after a long study. "An old woman is burned as a witch. 1943."

"Totally goofy!" Kenny shouted.

"They're having fun," Faye said to Gladys in the kitchen.

"He's painting her house," Gladys said, lighting up a cigarette.

"Yeah, I guess he doesn't think Eve is alive anymore."

"He's forgotten for the moment. Took him a long time. She was that special."

"Eve was? I didn't know her too well. I was a teen acher when she died."

"Dead is dead is what I say," Gladys said.

"Oh, my, who are you fooling?" Antony said, stepping out of nowhere. "As if you weren't living with that dead Sweeney all these years."

"Aren't you on the fryer, Antony? Well, Pay attention to that."

"I'm done frying. I'm going out there and make sure that poor fool knows he can live with the living and the dead."

"What's that mean?" Faye asked, but Antony was out to the bar.

Antony abruptly put fresh drinks in front of Lorna and Kenny and then stood there looking at them.

"I know you," Lorna said. "You cut the hedges into cute shapes."

"Topiary is one of my jobs," Antony said." I'm the town's topiarist."

"Lorna, this is Antony. Man of all jobs. Bartending now I guess."

Antony nodded and held his ground, staring at the two of them.

"You have something to tell us?" Kenny asked.

"Yes, I do. It is always magic. The living and the dying. Deep mystery. When whom you love has been with you far beyond recall, you get when they are gone to feel the mystery. Because for you they've not gone. They can't be you think. But they are. But only in the most superficial way. Nothing hides the terror of life more than this."

"Goofy," Kenny said. "I don't know what you're saying Antony but I never really do. Now's more goofy than usual."

"Well, I hear you, Antony," Lorna said.

"Ok. You're on his goofy wave length," Kenny said.

"I don't think the ones we love who have died want us to live as if we too were dead. We can live and not leave them. We can do two impossible things at once. Lewis Carroll."

Kenny pushed away from the bar.

"I can drive you back to your place but I got to get up early tomorrow. Paint don't wait."

"I'm going to stay for a bit," Lorna told him, caught by surprise at his abruptness.

"Okay. See you. Got four more bedrooms to paint. It was good. Goofy but good."

"You can advise me on what to do with seven bedrooms."

"Make it a boarding house," Kenny said, not knowing what he was saying but wanting out.

"I have never seen Kenny get nervous like that," Antony said as they watched Kenny go out the door.

"Can I get another, Antony? Pour one for yourself."

"Complimenti," Antony said, raising his glass of Polish vodka. "Ad Eva, morta tanto tempo fa. Tanto tempo fa."

"You speak Italian?' she said and yet not surprised by this man of all work.

"I speak some different words in different places. It's how I get by."

She laughed.

"I've listened to your radio broadcast. You seem to know what's going on around here. Tell me, does Kenny's daughter know her mother's dead?"

"Cissy? We all called her Pancakes. She grew up playing in those woods and catching toads and such in the bog. And seeing stuff."

Lorna waited.

"So?"

"So? So, she ain't too clear on who's dead and who's not."

That, Lorna figured, finishing her drink, would end the night.

"The dead don't know they're dead but the living know they're not dead."

"Epicurus."

"Nothing in between?" she asked, this man of all work.

"Maybe Founder," Antony said, after a moment.

In the middle of that night, Freddie got a call from Kenny.

"It's unbelievable to me that she could have died," Kenny said by way of an hello and an apology for calling at 3AM. "Sometimes at night from her side of the bed I hear her voice. She's excited: 'Boy! I'm alive!' She called me Boy when we were first married."

"Yeah, I know Kenny. Go back to sleep. We gotta finish that job. I want that one to be over, you know what I mean?"

"She wants to know what to do with seven bedrooms."

"Boarding house."

"That's what I told her. Good night, Freddie."

No one knew when Tristan Magistus's radio broadcast, now sandwiched between Antony's *Gnostic* broadcast and Rev. Goodnow's *Dead Words*, first showed up but it was now popular in the Encampment, broadcast through a few speakers throughout the camp that Moran had set up with Antony's help.

Tristan had a great radio voice, a mix of Richard Burton saying "Sea Wife, we need to talk" and the Almighty voice echoing Charlestown Headstone from behind a burning bush.

"Let's just say for starters, to get the ball rolling tonight, sort of a late night launch, a *Genesis* so to speak, and I'm coming to make this clear later on why I begin here and not later on and why when the show's over, curtain comes down and I say The End that you say to yourself, that would have made a better beginning when in fact the heart of magic, or what you could say its essence, the soul of it, maybe a punch line or the bottom line that closes the deal is, in point of fact, is to show the beginning in one hand while hiding the end in the other.

I've already begun so let's get to the meat of the matter.

Which all comes down to what I've seen in walking around these woods here behind the *Founder Asylum* and *Bageleria,* as well as early morning dives into the bog at all hours of the day and night.

The point here is that everything, regardless of whether it has a face and talks, or like an opossum has opposable thumbs on their back feet, is part of the Plan. Now, here's the magic part. Thinginess is part of the Plan but because Thinginess can't plan, it doesn't know animal crackers about the Plan.

Bog Iron. I repeat. Bog Iron. I think everyone now living but not living by any definition that people not living in the Encampment would see as living, these people should suck out all the Bog Iron they can, load it in Sonny's LamB, and sell it to *Founder Factor* in a barter for food and gas. Gas will be needed to get out of town.

That being said, Bog Iron can tell me nothing about the Plan of which it is a part. Bog boggy muddy flora and fauna can't tell me anything about the Plan though they are part of the Plan.

The Plan is in the, so to speak, Things but also the birds and the bees, the flowers and the trees, the wind and the air, the sea and the shore, the cats and rats, the snakes and bats, the fish and bugs. They can't say a word about the Plan but they're in it. They don't know it.

Now, as a magician of long-time union membership when I meet those with faces who can walk and talk, they all have a plan. There's as many plans as there are people. The best laid plans of men and women jump the guard rails. Elsewhere, the Plan of mice doesn't ever screw them over. You'll never find a mouse who's depressed or bored or anxious, devious or blood thirsty.No mouse is a son of a bitch. But you walk around the Encampment and you bump into them, sometimes they're a swarm. People. You go to a wake and you think everybody there is thinking "Wow? Death is the Plan." But they're not thinking that. They're thinking that sorry son of a bitch in the casket got the short end of the stick. No mouse thinks like that. They all know their days are numbered. They fearlessly go for the cheese in the trap they clearly see.

Look, fellow Campers, I know I won't get the short end of the stick because I'm a fucking Magician. Trismegistus. Who dat? Listen up, listeners and fellow Campers. The Greeks picked up from the Egyptians that there was a god called Thoth who symbolized wisdom and learning, and the Greeks named him Hermes Trismegistus, or "thrice greatest Hermes" because their guy Hermes was already the psychopomp, or "soul guide", who led the dead to the underworld, which they called Hades. This thrice loaded dude described the material world as well as the quest for spiritual perfection.

I'm in line with that guy according to Ancestry.com. Tell me this is not pure genius. This is a sentence you need to take home, take to the bank, ponder and pillage: "That which is below is like that which is above and that which is above is like that which is below to do the miracles of one only thing and as all things have been and arose from one by the mediation of one, so all things have their birth from this one thing by adaptation."

If you can handle that, call or write.

Now, you walk into *Sweeney's* and they're in there, drinking coffee. Sorry sons of bitches, numbnuts and jackwads are walking and shooting their mouths off all over town.

I met The Founder. Something like a run in. Magic skills in play which I can't reveal unless you kill me. The Founder? He's that stone in front of *The Founder Gasthaus* with the name "The Founder" carved on it. I'll tell you something. If a Founder is a founder of a hashwit dynasty or a buggy ship factory or whatever around to found, he's a sorry son of a bitch because when he fucks up it's because you can't do your job, or you're too dumb to see how his fuck ups are really part of the plan.

I say he because I can never, ever see myself calling a woman a sorry son of bitch. And I'm a magician. All you campers freezing your asses out here and spooning into a communal pot of beans made by Antony know if it wasn't for the Sun and a Woman, we wouldn't be any place at all.

Was he a sorry son of a bitch, you ask me? The Founder? In situations like this, I always ask "What's your plan?" Ok. That sucks. I mean your plan. It most likely leaves out "I'm going to cash out some day, maybe sweetly drugged in hospice, or maybe I'll drop dead like two hundred pounds of sand suddenly ran out of me. Kids don't have a plan. You can give them shit, nannies, a smartphone, a trip to Dizzyland, but they're receiving gifts. Instead of a plan they have fears and illusions.

Let me begin by saying that in a decade or so, they'll find you in your Encampment. Maybe the bones or maybe eating beans. They'll be more of you. More of the Dead will be roaming around. You'll have a sorry son of a bitch, descendant of the Founder. He'll have a plan. You'll think yours is better but what you think won't mean fuckall. On the good side, the bog and the woods will start talking back. Amen. Stay on the dial for Rev. Goodnow's *Dead Words* comes on next. You know he's dead, right?"

PART THREE

*"If the anger of the ruler rises against you, do not
leave your place
For calmness will lay great offenses to rest"*
Ecclesiastes 10:4

Let me go down the drive-way, say, a couple of hundred feet, to
the year *Bog Spa and Retreat featuring Hiking Trails and Hidden
Encampment,* Old *Sweeney's Gastropub, Hedge Fund Outdoor Drive-in
Theatre* behind the abandoned *Asylum,* and *The Rev. Goodnow
Scripture Garden,* and the *Old Iron Bog Mine* and other such
attractions laid a gloss on the town that paint couldn't rival.

Visitors showed up early at the Bog entrance to witness random
surfacing of bones which the archaeologists say date back to the
Cretaceous and some newer ones are scooped out and examined for
clues to a couple three murders that were perpetrated some years
ago. Visitors showed up they say to see things open up because the
woods behind the Bog and about a quarter of a mile from the old
Asylum are reputed to have within them in various places portals
to what's past. And the who and what back then. I don't mean the
rock n' roll band. In one day, some bones will hit the surface in the
morning and later on in the day in a stroll through the woods, you
just might run into whoever was wearing those bones when alive.

I'm not afraid to say that I've seen my own bones come out of
that bog and later eyeball me, former Sheriff Jake Wilcox, morel and
truffle searching in the woods. I'm puzzled to amazement by all this
but as I am not certain what my pre-birth life was or where exactly
I went when I was pronounced dead in my sleep at *Restorative Life,*

I'm kind of used to not knowing what is from what ain't, what's there behind what's here. Dr. Baconey told me not to worry because what I had was ordinary slippage. And up the driveway here, slippage is all of what's going on.

Now, my friends, I am opposed to the system of society in which we live today, not because I lack the natural equipment to do for myself, but because I am not satisfied to make myself comfortable knowing that there are thousands upon thousands of my fellow men who suffer for the barest necessities of life. We were taught under the old Cretaceous ethic that man's business upon this earth was to look out for himself. That was the ethic of the cave, the ethic of the wild beast. Take care of yourself; no matter what may become of your fellowman. Thousands of years ago the question was asked: "Am I my brother's keeper?" That question has never yet been answered in a way that is satisfactory to civilized society. Yes, I am my brother's keeper."

"Is that Moran again? Where is he broadcasting from?"

Williams shook his head.

"He moves around. They can't find him. Probably the woods."

"How can a fugitive from the police be running for president?"

"Jesus was a carpenter."

"Good analogy," Earhart responded. "You once said Moran was a devil."

"A fallen angel."

"So where did that fallen angel get that line of weep? He doesn't believe a word of it. Isn't he a fan of that Atlas Drugged woman? Eye Round? The 'Get the Hell out of my way' philosopher?"

"No. It's not her. He's reading a speech Eugene Debits gave in 1908. He was running for president. He ran for president four times and lost. The last time he was in prison under sedition charges. He became ill in prison and died soon after his sentence was commuted by Warren G. Hardon."

"So, Moran is now a socialist and also a fallen angel?"

Of course, he didn't answer. Earhart had come to know that Johnny evaded the concrete and evoked the numinous. Reading Rudolph Otto didn't help.

Something she didn't want to admit had lately been creeping in when she thought about the success, the weird cultish devotion to Johnny. The last copy of *The Founder Courier* was in the Smithsonian probably. She should be in there too. Stuffed with a sign saying "Extinct Local Newspaper Reporter." She had settled into being a "Content Provider" for a twelve year old kid that, a real turn of the screw, was her daughter, Persephone's, favorite Influencer. But that gig was scheduled for extinction as the newest AI worked up content from all data available algorithmically targeting the psyche of humans under the age of 18. On one hand, she thought that she was writing the content that was influencing her own daughter, a kind of indirect manner of child rearing, which was good, but on the other hand and fucking perverse as all hell, she had a shit relationship with her daughter who saw her as an embittered, unenlightened person of no joy. Of course, she worshipped Johnny, the Perfect Dad. She seemed to understand him which was something she, the unenlightened person of no joy, of course could not understand that. She should follow the 12 year old Influencer of all knowing and learn how to live.

Talking to Johnny about this scene from Hades brought no relief.

"They are not using my content," Earhart told him, trying to stay calm. "They call what I give them fodder that will trigger the 12 year's natural talent for reaching a demographic that is more volatile, superficial and brutal than Caligula. The little bitch fucks up everything I write. She turns it into a mean mush of hate speech. Spite is what she sells. And our daughter is buying it."

His answer to that?

"I couldn't love you the way I do if I didn't know and feel what living without knowing you, without loving you was like."

She absolutely didn't have a clue as to how to connect what he said to the real absolutely infuriating situation she was facing with her daughter. Their daughter.

"Does what you just said have something to do with Eve?"

"Eve never died. It wasn't because the writers didn't care about her. She brought Death and Sin into the world. Why chronicle her death they concluded. Best forgotten. But, no. She never died, never was buried but is born again in every woman born."

"Maybe her bones will float up at the Bog Spa and give the tourists a real thrill."

"Our Persephone. The Goddess of Spring. Never death."

That was always the way it went. The way it ended. She thought about going to Baconey with all of these issues but he didn't take insurance, not that she had any, and his forty minute session charge was exorbitant. It did look like those walking the streets or wandering in the woods with blankets over their shoulders, sometimes dragging their goods in stolen shopping carts, were more addled than the wealthy with beds and roofs but Baconey told her that the wealthy were addled too. Just differently. There were existentially threatening psychoses and then there was the non-existentially threatening. The Outdoorsy type perished by starvation, septic wounds, exposure, ticks, snakes, scorpions, filthy water, and lack of sleep way before any psychosis killed them. Those accustomed to living indoors and sleeping in a bed had their hypochondria tended to the way their masseuse tended to their bodies. They were doomed to live long lives fearful that they wouldn't find the right shrink to show them how to unite with themselves in love of themselves.

Moran did no more than two broadcasts from the cooler at *Sweeney's* before changing location. Klaus was his sound engineer, a damn good engineer Moran thought, though Klaus in his '90s was hearing challenged.

Moran was straightening shit on the crate he put his mic on while Klaus was tinkering with the transmitter.

"What's it going to be today, Moran?" Faye Fata asked, standing by the doorway. "Damn, we're going to lose our butter and perishable in here at this temp. What did you raise it to?"

"Klaus gets a chill and my voice freezes to a cackle. You want me to win this election, don't you, Faye?"

"The Presidency of the United States of America? Fuck no. You're a bat out of hell with a rabies bite. Besides, you're not on any ballot in the country. You've got no funding."

"That's just your opinion," Klaus growled. "He's got backers."

"You won't get on any ticket," Faye said, smiling. "What's your party? Where are your big doners? Where's your organization."

"Ownership has changed you," Moran told her. "You are now part of a different alliance than Klaus and myself. You have aligned yourself with revel, luxury and riot. Ownership has destroyed your humanity. And there was a time, I loved you, a far better you, my dear Faye."

"Well, that far better me turned you down. What? Four times."

Just then, Klaus cued Moran who grabbed his mic.

In every age of this world's history, the kings and emperors and czars and the potentates, in alliance with the priests, have sought by all the means at their command to keep the people in darkness that they might perpetuate the power in which they riot and revel in luxury while the great mass are in a state of slavery and degradation, and he who has spoken out courageously against the existing order, he who has dared to voice the protest of the oppressed and down-trodden, has had to pay the penalty, all the way from Jesus Christ of Galilee to Fred Warren of Girard."

"Who the hell is Fred Warren of Girard?" Gladys asked Faye later as they sat in a booth drinking coffee.

"I don't know but he's on the Jesus level according to Moran."

"I shouldn't let that little prick back there," Gladys said angrily.

"Moran?"

"The other one. Klaus. Like father like son."

Faye thought about that. It seemed that sometimes Gladys' Alzheimer didn't kick in and then other times it did.

A crew of tourists came noisily in and Antony went over to take their orders.

"Further still living in his car?" Gladys asked.

"Further? No, he's got a room over at the boarding house Kenny is running. He works here now. You hired him back tend bar."

"Those people are getting on my nerves," Gladys said loud enough to be heard by all.

"Who's the disgruntled madame?" one of the tourists asked Antony.

"That's Sweeney," Antony told him. "She's at war with change."

"Except if you're old you want to change back to being young."

They all laughed.

"Tell them to order, eat and get out," Gladys called out.

"Let's go for a walk," Faye said. "It's nice out."

"I'd rather stay here and remember."

She closed her eyes and Faye guessed she was doing just that. Remembering.

"I've seen you on TV. You interview people."

"He does? You're kidding."

"It's one of those . . "

Antony saw them rushing out of their Hummers. *Bog Spa Private Security.* The woods people called them Pisswater Security. They had full SQUAT gear on and F-16 rifles.

"Oh, my," Antony said. "Don't shoot us."

"Where is he?" one of the commandos shouted.

"Is this real?"

"Very."

Moran and Klaus were out of the cooler and headed to the back door but shots rang out and they stopped.

Both men were thrown to the ground and hands cuffed behind their back and then both lifted.

"I'm running for the presidency," Moran told them. "I am campaigning. This is not a crime."

"You're broadcasting obscene and inflammatory speech over the airwaves."

"Treasonous and incendiary."

"I want a lawyer," Klaus sputtered angrily. "I'll be fucked if I'm gonna be arrested by corporate cops."

One of the corporate cops hit Klaus with his rifle butt. Klaus screamed.

"I got it on my phone!" one of the tourists yelled and she and her friends rushed out the door.

"This will go to court," Faye yelled, as Moran and Klaus were bum rushed out the door and then into a Hummer.

"I don't want those two in here again," Gladys said as Faye went back to her.

"I don't think we have a court," Antony said, sitting down with them.

Gladys looked at him.

"You knew Sweeney didn't you Robert?"

"No, I don't know either of them."

"What do you mean we don't have a court?" Faye asked. "And this is Antony. Not Robert, whoever he is."

"There is a court now but it is not a court that any court that was a real court would say is a court."

"Fuck me," Faye exclaimed, an eyes wide look at Antony. Sometimes this guy really troubled her.

They sat and smoke and drank coffee for another hour or so and then Antony turned on the radio.

"I wish to say in the broadest possible way that I am opposing the system under which we live today because I believe it is subversive of the best interests of the people. I am not satisfied with things as they are, and I know that no matter what administration is in power, even were it a Socialist administration, I know that there will be no material change in the condition of the people until we have a new social system based upon the mutual economic interest of the people."

"Don't tell me," Faye said, shaking her head in utter disbelief.

"Moran," Antony said. "He's not the kind of human you can tie up and throw in a Hummer and expect it to go well."

It's not a classical physics but a quantum trip to go ahead on the road of time to where Kenny Ramakrishna owned and lived in the Italian Marvel with seven bedrooms that Lorna Neelye had left him in her will, she having drowned on a lee shore off the coast of Croatia. Such a beginning is both unexpected and tragic but within the tradition of causality originating in Aristotle's Physics and Metaphysics. It becomes a quantum trip which I can't measure from outside the quantum world and it's of no use to try to put into words in a causal world of non-contradiction how this came about. I mean that the boarders: Lucy Powell, Sonny Bone, Further Fada, Oedipus Baconey, Cissy Ramakrishna, F. Gregory Coletti and Antony Scipio Nicodemus had in no way planned to be among such an incompatible collective but indeed were here living together nonetheless.

Suffice it to say on this evening at the Italian Marvel just above bog ground that Kenny had named, in Lorna's memory, *Casa Lorna,* Antony and Lucy were laying platters of chicken on both ends of the Italian Marble dining room table. Then they sat down, Antony at one end of the table closest to the kitchen.

"You need to park that LamB either in the garage or definitely not in the middle of the drive," Further said to Sonny Bone, the two sitting across from each other.

"It doesn't start," Sonny said sullenly, passing the mashed potatoes to Cissy who sat to his left. "I mean maybe sometimes it starts. And sometimes it doesn't."

"Then junk it and get it off the property," Further told him.

"As if this property belonged to you."

'Oh, fuck me," Further moaned. "We gonna hear how your Daddy owned all this and was swindled by Specter?"

"Who's Spectre?" Lucy asked.

"He could be referring to a villainous organization in the James Bond movies," Baconey pointed out, "or simply pointing out that the villain here is a ghost. A spectre. Delusionals all have spectres in their psyche."

"I know it was Moran," Sonny told Baconey. "Maybe it was him. It was somebody."

"They came for Moran at *Sweeney's* where he was broadcasting socialist propagation. I was there."

"Did he put up a fight?" Sonny asked.

"No, he did not. But he escaped soon after and was broadcasting again."

"He's done a couple from here, hasn't he, Dad?"

"Yeah. He and Klaus set up in the attic."

All eyes were turned to Kenny who sat at the head of the table. No one asked why Kenny let Klaus and Moran use the attic.. There was something about Kenny that had changed noticeably. He didn't seem to find anything goofy any longer. He seemed confused most of the time. Baconey said it was early onset dementia. Lucy thought Lorna's death had traumatized him. His hair had turned white like Moses's Lucy claimed. Cissy had told F. Gregory that her father no longer talked to her mother, Eve.

"Had he always done that?"

"Yes. As if she never died."

She had seen that 'this is so crazy" look on his face. All that was another reason why she felt that F. Gregory and Lucy Powell just didn't jive, in spite of the fact that he had told Lucy he had come back to Founder to find what he had run from. His therapist had told him that unless he faced what he feared, his mind would never clear. If part of what he had run from was Lucy, he didn't say. He also seemed much changed having spent the last 16 months in some institution that Lucy just figured was a Nerve Farm. He had left his hedge fund, *The Schrodinger Fund,* to auto-AI operation and seemed not to be concerned as to what the hell was going on. Sometimes Cissy saw in him the same look that her father had in his eye as did Williams, what Lucy Powell had called Dulcinea fix. Working pro bono had brought Lucy to her as a client more than once and they had become close friends. Lucy's run in with the law were mostly the civil disobedience misdemeanor sort but sentencing had toughened since the town judicial system was now appointees and not elected.

The conversation now was on the hired mercenaries that had replaced the Sheriff's office.

"Jake would be turning over in his grave," Further said.

That angered Lucy.

"Jake is not below ground," she said vehemently, pointing her fork at Further. She wanted to vote him out of *Casa Lorna* but as yet she knew she didn't have the votes.

"Okay. They sunk him in the bog."

She wanted to get up and go smack him but instead she threw her knife at him which flew passed his head.

"Hey, calm down," Further cried out. "Baconey what's her problem?"

Baconey looked at Lucy. He was about to render a verdict when Kenny said:

"She's a daughter of fair Eve."

"Thank you, Kenny," Lucy said.

A hush fell over the table.

"You know, Dad, you are getting to sound a lot like Williams. Don't you think so, Dr. Baconey?"

Baconey seemed surprised by this address.

"I can't say anything about my analysands."

"Him or Earhart?" Cissy asked sharply.

"Oh, my!" Antony exclaimed. "Aren't you the lawyer at cross."

"You know why Cissy didn't become a Wealth Adviser?" Further asked the table. "Because she doesn't know anybody that's wealthy and they don't know her."

Nobody laughed along with him.

"Your Dad gave all his wealth to some foreigners in Greece," Sonny said.

"What do you say I go out there and take a sledge hammer to your LamB," Further shot back.

"This man here sounds like he should join up with the *Founder Mercenaries of Street Safety.*"

"You're the one cozy with those guys."

"I have interviewed a pair of them on my show," Antony said.

"I saw that," Lucy said, giggling. "They said they need to bring some people to order so other people can go on with their lives. Or something like that. They said they had names and faces."

"I agree with that," Further said. "Like some people who throw knives...."

"It was a butter knife, you baby."

"There's a surveillance camera every one hundred feet now looking in every direction."

"There's paranoia right there," Further said.

"I am merely making an observation," Baconey told him.

"They are rounding up the tent people out in the woods," Sonny told them. "Maybe. The Encampment. It's the people sleeping in their cars parked on the streets. Not in the woods. And anybody walking around in the rain with a wet blanket over their heads. Walking in the streets. Maybe some of them. And the Encampment."

He paused.

"I'm just glad you let me stay here, Kenny."

"Yeah, where the hell are you working, Sonny Boy?"

"You're eating right now what this man worked on," Antony told Further.

"Okay. Glad to hear it. It's good. Sonny here and me. Destined to inherit millions and now he's frying spuds and I'm pouring shots at *Sweeney's.*"

"Did Gladys sign the place over to Faye? I mean your sister is running it."

"They got some kind of arrangement. Gladys is developing cheese brain real quick."

"You are so much less than three fifths of a human being, Further. You never went further than an amoeba."

"Cissy, your Dad is here so..."

"Cissy is a beautiful daughter of Eve, Further."

Kenny's words froze the table once again.

"Sure, Kenny," Further said, clearing his throat. "You are correct, sir."

"A minion of the new order came yesterday," Antony said, as Further and Baconey got up to clear the table. "He wanted Faye to put up a sign that read "We Own Everything So You Don't Have To!"

"And who's the We?" Lucy asked, rolling herself a cigarette.

"The Royal We," Antony said. "The Owners. *Bog Spa & Retreat* own a lot but almost all of what was public is in the hands of private management. You can trace who owns that to a private equity firm. I had someone on their Team on my show. Or will have if I'm not hit with an injunction against running the tape of the interview. It happened with my interview with a gentleman who gave me an account of hunting possum with Mike Woad. Our dead Mike Woad. The Team or The Owners, or both, argued that such an interview would incite mental disturbances, frighten tourists from visiting the Bog Spa, confound the peace and tranquility of the living, and subvert the Abrahamic Covenant regarding where the dead go."

"Who's on dish washing tonight?" Further yelled from the kitchen.

It was way past midnight and Lucy was out on the porch, which was huge and swept around the entire front of *Casa Lorna,* when F. Gregory appeared out of the darkness.

"F. Gregory," Lucy giggled when she saw him.

"Please. It's Frankie, Jr. I came here to find the me that I was before F. Gregory."

She offered him her cigarette makings.

"I don't smoke."

"Frankie, Jr did."

He nodded and took the pouch from her.

She lit him up. They sat listening to the cicadas, tree frogs and Cretaceous grunts.

"Was it terrible bad for you in that rehab?" she asked. "Did they fry your brains to make you normal?"

Something about that excited her he thought. She was ...different.

"Mostly drug regimen?"

"We talked a lot. My therapists and me."

"How many did you have? Did you have to take the Baconey test? You know, what do you think other people are, what objects do you have relations with, where do you think time past goes, and, let me see, what lies do you tell yourself about yourself. I'm paraphrasing. Why are you laughing?"

"I'm not. I know what therapy you're referring to. I had that."

"So, did I. Did you pass? Dr. Baconey said I would pass if I were on a different planet."

This time he laughed outright.

"Why are you laughing?" she said angrily.

"Please forgive me but let me laugh. It's been so long. It's so good being with you. You're a joyful presence. Like infinity. Zeno imagined infinity. He used paradox to display ideas."

"Okay, I guess. I wish I could say I like being with you. You know you're not joyful?"

"Don't be angry. I think I'll be better."

"So, did you pass or not?"

"I couldn't work up much enthusiasm for any of it. There was a neo-post-Freudian that wanted me to talk a lot about my mother. He seemed to think that she was at the root of whatever happened to me. He kept on like that even after I told him she had died before I could talk."

Lucy didn't think that sounded right.

"I was over your house and met her. We were both in high school. So, she was around to hear you talk for quite a few years."

She took her pocket flask out of her buckskin jacket and took a slug and then handed it to Frankie Jr.

"Take a slug and refresh your memory."

He did as was told.

"Wasn't your mother's name Zoe, a.k.a Eve? Cissy told me that. She studied Eve in law school."

She giggled so hard she sputtered her vodka.

"I made that up. But she's an expert on the name."

Now, she was getting out there in the woods and in the bog where his grandfather and his hunting dog could appear, where former Sheriff Jake Wilcox was lying there still alive, where three unsolved murders had been perpetrated, where his own father was shot and calling to him.

He sort of crumpled visibly and she put her arms around him.

"Hey, Frankie, you're with me. You said you wanted to be with me. I'm here. Remember the crazy time we had at the Prom? I mean I was certifiable and you out of kindness went along with it."

He looked up at her and took her face between both hands.

"You're not certifiable. You never were. You're lovely."

When he kissed her, it felt like the first time he solved a Diophantine Equation.

Later on, in her room, she heard Kenny calling for Eve. And she knew for sure Frankie Jr had Eve issues. Deep, deep Eve issues. She saw that she could catch some last minutes of Rev. Goodnow's *Dead Voices* broadcast:

"And I said, 'He who hears, let him get up from the deep sleep.' And he wept and shed tears. Bitter tears he wiped from himself and he said, 'Who is it that calls my name, and from where has this hope come to me, while I am in the chains of the prison?' And I said, 'I am the Pronoia of the pure light; I am the thinking of the virginal Spirit, who raised you up to the honored place. Arise and remember that it is you who hearkened, and follow your root, which is I, the merciful one, and guard yourself against the angels of poverty and the demons of chaos and all those who ensnare you, and beware of the deep sleep and the enclosure of the inside of Hades."

When Cissy showed up at the *Founder Public Defenders' Office* Monday morning, she was surprised to find the whole place in frenetic activity. Besides the staff shoveling stuff from their desks into boxes there were a number of uniformed *armed Founder Mercenaries of Street Protection* standing menacingly against the walls. She saw that the names of the Chief Public Defender and Assistant Public Defender had been blacked out.

"What's going on?" she asked the first person's whose attention she could get. Everyone seemed to be running for their lives.

"We've been shut down."

"What? By who?"

One of the Street Protector's came up to her.

"If you work here, Miss, you need to take whatever is yours and clear out."

"I can't. I need to appear in Court."

That made him smile.

"Well, you can't appear at a place that no longer exists. You'll get a letter of explanation but right now you need to do what I say and leave."

"I need to represent my client in a preliminary hearing to show cause. The clock is running on this."

"The clock is running on you leaving or you will be detained for a real cause – obstructing a police action."

"Oh, give me a break. You are private mercenaries. There's no law on your side. Posse Comitatus is not lawful. It's unlawful for you thugs to be attempting to close down a legal Public Defender's Office. An elected office."

"Elections are over. If this guy has been elected, he's de-elected as of now. No authority. And what you call the public is bullshit. Now, last time, leave peacefully or we'll pull you in."

"To where?" Cissy said angrily. "Don't tell me. Of course, we still have places to incarcerate."

It still caught her by surprise when she was spun around and handcuffed. On her way out she saw Patti on her desk, a bit worse for wear, looking sad. Tears came. She wished she could be Pancakes again and protect Patti.

"Comrades and fellow-soldiers, we have here met with an encounter, and they are ten times in number more than we. Shall we charge them or no? "

Kenny and Freddie stopped painting and looked at Moran, who had just rushed into the parlor they were painting a shade below Emerald Green for Mrs. Nutt, widow of *Nutt's Hardware Store*.

"What are you raving about Moran?" Freddie said, noting that Moran was dressed like some sort of pirate.

"Alas, mates, our shipmate, Klaus has been captured."

"Don't lean on that wall," Freddie hollered.

"Who captured who?" Kenny asked, re-focusing on his painting."

"Exactly who are you going to charge?" Freddie asked. "When did you become a pirate? I don't see a boat."

"A ship, sir. A boat goes on a ship. A ship cannot go on a boat."

"You don't have either one, do you?"

"This is a mystery, mates," Moran said taking off a smashed fedora he was wearing and wiping his brow. "The truth is Klaus is missing."

"From where?" both brothers asked.

"From where? Good question. From where he was."

"Which is?"

"He wasn't with me. That's the truth. I haven't seen the Quartermaster for. What's today?"

"And the Quartermaster is?"

"Klaus."

"Ok, Moran. Get out of here. We got to finish this job."

"I can see that," Moran said, nodding. "I came by to see if you might have a berth for your mate here at *Casa Lorna*. My ship went down on a lee shore."

"Sounds like bullshit."

"What's today? Tuesday. She went down a week ago today."

"We're full up at *Casa Lorna*," Kenny told him.

"I was informed that there was a vacancy."

"Who told you that?" Kenny asked.

"Klaus."

Freddie laid his brush down.

"I'm going out for a breath. You can go down this rabbit hole, bro."

Moran nodded as Freddie walked past him and out the door.

Moran lit a cigarette.

"You can't smoke in here."

"I know. That would be the wee smallest charge brought against me. Klaus isn't the only one missing."

Kenny was thinking about vacancies and the only one missing so deeply all of a sudden that he smeared his edge. He put the brush down.

"Was Klaus talking about Eve?"

"Would that be your Eve or Johnny's Eve? Or going way back, that fair Eve who was the mother of us all?"

Kenny stared at him blankly.

"If you want to know the truth of it," Moran said, blowing smoke upward into the new ceiling paint. An off yellow. "Klaus was hauled off on our last encounter with the Proud Thuggees. Month or so ago. I'm putting together a small rescue crew to board that ship."

Kenny didn't reply.

Moran studied the man closely.

"You know truth here is I don't have a problem with Klaus being missing. Two people in that Asylum who were certifiable. Klaus was one. We hang together but between me and you, the guy is a Louie. It's a sad thing."

Kenny didn't seem to be paying attention.

"If you ask who the other certifiable is, it's Johnny Williams. But you didn't ask, did you?"

Kenny remained frozen.

Moran flipped his cigarette butt on the parquet floor.

"Will you sign ship's articles, mate, and come aboard?"

"What? Oh, yeah."

"Grand!" Moran shouted as Kenny sort of drifted out of the room, wondering who was missing at the *Casa Lorna?*

"What bell is dinner, mate?" Moran called after him. "Corn is the sinews of war!"

"I don't know why you keep asking me about other people? Or what the time is?"

Baconey uncrossed and then crossed his legs again.

This lady, he forgot her name, sitting across from him and sharply questioning him should, if he had done things right, been lying on a couch and he should have been sitting behind her so that he couldn't see her and she couldn't see him. What he had now was this analysand's doubting eyes looking at him. The room should have also been darkened, the shades or curtains drawn, a mechanical clock ticking loudly. Instead, what he had was too much light, too much visibility all round. What was required when probing the dark recesses of unconscious was a dark room and a blurry distance between himself and the analysand. If he was to be a voice of the repressed regions of the unknowable, at least to consciousness, he had to be himself an avatar of that. Instead, what he had now with this woman, whose name he had forgotten, was laid out like a plate of eggs frying in a full sun.

"I think we'll lower the blinds a bit," Baconey said, getting up. "And…and I'm going to sit over here."

"Behind me? Am I talking to the wall now?"

"Madame, to reach…."

"Madame?"

"My dear, we need a light on what is unseen in you but not the light of the conscious mind. That is a barrier to where we want to go."

"I see. You darken the room and you sit where I can't see you."

"Exactly. We need to obscure that which is comfortable and familiar."

"You know you're acting funny, Dr. Baconey. You're making me very uncomfortable. I've read that therapists kill themselves at a much higher rate than ordinary, normal people. Someone told me your given name is Oedipus. He had a tragic end, didn't he?"

"You can lie on that couch if you wish."

"It would be more comfortable but you said I shouldn't be comfortable."

"Ah, but on the deepest level, you are not at all comfortable. Otherwise, you would not be here seeking my help."

"I thought I'd give it a try. Actually, I don't think there's anything wrong with me. Of course, I am surrounded by a confederacy of dunces, as they say, at my office. At *Bog Spa*. I would chop off all their heads is what I feel like doing sometimes. Is that unusual? The young ones especially. They think they'll always be a size O and no cat claws under their eyes. Well, the future will hit them like a fist to the face. If it wasn't for the absolutely wonderful collections of almost everything I have. Really, I have very little. I'm just fantasizing. I mean that I'm striking to look at. I am though, so that's not really a problem. Is that unusual? But, I am so attached to this ring I'm wearing. It's a symbol of my soul. I am, you know, Dr. Baconey, in possession of a soul so much like what you find in those torturous Russian novels."

She took a breath.

"Well, I feel so much better. Can I schedule?"

"With my assistant, if you please."

She smiled warmly as they shook hands.

"You're everything they said you were. Wonderful."

"Thank you so much."

He knew he should have said her name but he had forgotten it.

"He was wonderful," she told Antony as he looked to his laptop to schedule her another session.

"There's something *je ne sais quo pas* about him," she went on.

"That is what it is," Antony told her, handing her a card. "Next Tuesday. Nine AM. Mrs. Firewoad. Is that a branch of the Woad family?"

"Oh, no. That family is all dead. The Firewoads were here with The Founder. We don't seem to die. Is that unusual?"

"Well, Mike Woad is still living somewhere in the woods. And he's dead."

"Oh yes, he is. I've seen him. That's why I'm seeing Dr. Baconey. I shouldn't be seeing dead people, should I? I should have brought that up."

"You can do it next time, Mrs. Firewoad."

She thought about that on her way to the elevator.

Williams' podcast, *Overhearing*, had at first few followers but an anonymous grant kept it going until there was enough followers to attract sponsorships. And those sponsorships began to keep Williams and Earhart financially afloat. Her own podcast was the last vestige of *The Founder Chronicle* and while it too survived because of an anonymous grant it attracted only one sponsor – *Sweeney's Right Now Café* –and so Earhart knew she was dependent on Johnny. And she didn't want to be. She couldn't understand why her reportage, now on a weekly podcast, informing the citizens of Founder what was going on in their town, informing them of what they had to face and to deal with, informing them of what was changing outside their own niched worlds didn't seem important to them. Whereas what Johnny was doing was, well, just Johnny. It had nothing to do with what the hell was going on outside his head, which she had little idea what was going on in there. What came out gave no clues. It wasn't that a lot didn't come out but it was way outside, beyond, removed from the facts a rational mind would look for. And yet, fuck me she would scream to herself, he was a star in the town, a fucking celebrity. It was growing to cult like proportions. It was making her crazy. Seeing him around the apartment they had above *Sweeney's* following his daily routine: a long walk before sunrise, breakfast downstairs, which went on to lunch time because everyone who came in and saw him, townies new and old, Bog Spa tourists, people looking for directions, con artists, the hot tub set, mercenaries, and people who looked like people long dead – had to stop and chat with him. She had been with him for a decade and they never had anything like what she would call a chat. Talking to him made her perspire. But she was crazy about him. And he was crazy.

"You know who your fans are?" she asked him, one night just before he went to what he referred to as a "service," but not to pray as he wasn't a Christian, as far as she could make out, that any Christian would recognize.

"I'm going to Rev. Goodnow's *Some Day Eventual Holiness Apocalypse Church.*

"You mean the worshippers are your fans? I don't know them, you know."

"I don't either."

"Well, they are obviously on your wave length."

She wanted to say came from your planet.

"They tune in clearly to what you say," she tried again, noting that look a six year old gives you when the world baffles them.

"They do?"

"Yes, they do. It's an audience demographic. Like we knew the *Chronicle's* demographic was made up of readers, naturally, who could follow the movement of sentences and the building of paragraphs. You know, like the coherent development of a story. Or, a thought."

She paused and studied his attentive face, like a good pupil. He did have a face those he called astral presences probably had. Whoever and whatever they were. Such could be a stone or a twig she had learned. She had put down her Madame Blavatsky and Annie Besant and picked up Reality, Reason and Sanity long ago so learning something from Johnny meant un-learning everything she had previously ever learned.

"So, in short, our audience was comprised of literate people who also had a curiosity and an interest in knowing what perils might kill them that day, and who had died and why."

"I see."

"And then when that lot dwindled, we could no longer afford paper and ink. Or salaries. Remember when I told you that?"

'Yes, I do."

"So, I now make enough money with my podcast to buy chewing gum once a month. Which means your podcast is keeping us from living in the woods and sleeping in the trees. Or Sonny's LamB."

"It is?" he said, still bewildered.

"Yes, it is. That's why you need to know who your listeners are so that you continue, for our bills to be paid, to give them what they want. Otherwise, if it's just chance, you may lose the thread connecting you to them."

"The astral sympathy," he said, understanding.

"Yeah, well, I don't know what that is but you need to get to know who these fools, I mean, listeners are. Your audience. And Lord knows you've got a whole lot of those fuckers. I mean listeners."

She collapsed on the sofa. She hated herself for hating his listeners, for hating him for hating herself because she hated him and his listeners. Lately, she's had this feeling she'd like to kill all the idiots ruining her marriage. She shouldn't say marriage. Johnny seemed to think he was married but not to her. It was all envy. A guy who didn't know a fact from a nightmare, a guy whom she had seen talking to trees, stones and bees was going to survive while she, except for him, would be dead already.

And then he sat down next to her.

"I know," he told her.

He closed his eyes and recited:

"HERE ENTER NOT VILE BIGOTS, HYPOCRITES,

EXTERNALLY DEVOTED APES, BASE SNITES,

PUFFED-UP, WRY-NECKED BEASTS, WORSE THAN THE HUNS,

OR OSTROGOTHS, FORERUNNERS OF BABOONS:

CURSED SNAKES, DISSEMBLED VARLETS, SEEMING SANCTS,

SLIPSHOD CAFFARDS, BEGGARS PRETENDING WANTS,

FAT CHUFFCATS, SMELL-FEAST KNOCKERS, DOLTISH GULLS,

OUT-STROUTING CLUSTER-FISTS, CONTENTIOUS BULLS,

FOMENTERS OF DIVISIONS AND DEBATES,

ELSEWHERE, NOT HERE, MAKE SALE OF YOUR DECEITS.

HERE ENTER NOT ATTORNEYS, BARRISTERS,

NOR BRIDLE-CHAMPING LAW-PRACTITIONERS:

CLERKS, COMMISSARIES, SCRIBES, NOR PHARISEES,

"Fuck me," was all she could say.

"Rabelais," he told her, kissing her gently.

Yeah, she thought, there was something definitely going on with her Johnny and whatever it was didn't stop or pass Go.

"This is an audio podcast of *The Founder Chronicle*, Earhart Hearder, the last reporter of *The Chronicle* reporting thanks to the support of an anonymous donor who may be the last supporter of The Fourth Estate. Google it. It's not a real estate development.

There was a shoot-out behind the former *Founder Asylum* at the north end of the bog. The shoot-out was between Klaus Birke's *Jolly Joans*, in pirate costumes, sabers and pistols, and the *Hellfire Boys*, AR-15s and MK-47s.

Combatants on both sides were arrested by the *Founder Mercenaries of Street Safety* and held for arraignment at *God Knows Where*, which is where loved ones of the missing are seeking the missing.

What this reporter heard at *Sweeney's Café* was that a Mr. BahBah, pronounced blahblah, came before The Team to make the case that as he was the only living descendant of Founder's Founder all properties now managed by The Team should be signed over to him. The Team voted to pass whatever evidence Mr. BahBah had for his astounding claim over to *Private Predatory*. Investigative research this reporter had done previously had revealed an organizational chart in which *Private Predatory* was owned by an anonymous Panamanian shell company. This was a dead end as no public information was available to determine ownership identity.

Gladys Farquason, owner of the café and a longtime resident of *Founder* revealed to this reporter that the Hedge Fund behind Private Equity had been in her café. It was, in her words, the guy behind the guy behind that guy. She insisted this person's name was Hedge Fund and no amount of explanation on my part could clarify the matter for her. She is losing her grip on what's real in Founder and what ain't.

As of this moment this opaque ownership owns more than 50%

of all property in Founder, including the *Bog Spa and Retreat*, and *Founder Bog Iron* and *Bog Better Butter* managed by The Team who apparently rotate with other Teams elsewhere. None seem to be inhabitants of Founder.

Elections so far have been heavily swayed by funding from *Private Predatory*, which, if what Gladys Farquason reported is true, is itself funded by Mr. Hedge Fund, which is not an individual of that name this reporter is looking for because this reporter wants to stay out of a collapsing mind.

In other news, my own mate and partner, Johnny Williams, believes that an astral connection exists between himself and half this town's population who watch his video podcast.

You'll have to watch yourself for clarification for I can't offer a stitch. I try to limit this sort of conversation with Johnny for the sake of our marriage and my sanity.

Somewhat along the same lines of the astral and spectral, tourists roaming the woods and spa continue to report sightings of spectral figures who elude Smart phone capture. What are being called Frankenstein bodies pop up and disappear regularly if tourist reports can be believed.

What in years past was called The Encampment, the home in the woods of those who enjoyed living outdoors and those who had no choice, continues to be a major attraction at the Spa, which now has a $15 dollar entrance fee but no longer any inhabitants, rounded up long ago for arraignment.

For the sake of public safety, this reporter once again points out that bogs are not marshes or wetlands as bogs have low oxygen and chemicals released by sphagnum moss. Although there is a mud bath concession, a mud bath in the bog will not do you any good.

All this being said, bogs are reported to have a magical power to preserve organic material sunk into it. This is not a fountain of youth. Old people who jump in will die and not come out young.

On a brighter note, small deposits of gold can be found in the bog. On this bog matter finally, I need to report that my husband, Willams but I call him Johnny, believes that there are direct emanations of astral presences in Nature and that there is an internal knowledge in the bog and the Asylum Fossil Woods that can be overheard.

I'm reading from my notes taken in conversation with my Johnny. Stars, bogs, herbs and bees have some sort of sympathy with the astral that we can attach ourselves to, like we ride into a …wait, I'm reading… into an invisible super-elemental part of the un-created through Nature. We humans have both a carnal elemental body and an astral one, so we can tune in to … I guess what doesn't have a body.

Okay. I realize I've left factual reporting far behind and that if I have any listeners to this podcast, they won't at all be Johnny's listeners. Yes, I do find him spooky but what can I say? He's a great success here in Founder while I'm heading for a recycling bin. I can no longer juice reality out of what's going on here. Apologies. On an end note. Mr. BahBah speaks the language of The Founder which he says is Foundeese and he alone speaks it. I remarked that there is no private one person only language. That would be baby drivel. Mr. BahBah said "No."

Thank you

For the third night in a row, Cissy Ramakrishna had not appeared at *Casa Lorna*. And the search for her was not going well.

Tonight, Freddy sat in Kenny's place at the head of the table, and Moran, wearing a black eye patch over one eye sat in Cissy's seat.

"He never eats much," Freddy said in response to Lucy Powell's worry that Kenny was not eating.

No one at the table had seen Kenny since they had discovered Cissy was missing. Moran had put himself in charge of the search, mobilizing his former Encampment comrades.

"Kenny has been searching for Eve, I believe," Baconey said, passing chicken parts to Further.

He said this timidly, knowing any mention of Eve was verboten.

"Nothing to do with this," Freddy said, sharply.

That sharpness of tone was new coming from Freddy who was forever mild and courteous with everyone.

The table became absorbed in the baked chicken parts, Brussel sprouts and spuds.

"Don't you have anything to say?" Lucy said angrily to F. Gregory or sat across from her. "Can't you put that big brain to work and find Kenny and Cissy?"

F. Gregory dropped the bit of potato on the edge of his fork. He was suddenly the focus.

"I …I think Sheriff Wilcox would have been a great help here," he managed to say.

"Oh, my God!" Lucy said. "We need to send a man dead for

what....ten years out to look for Cissy? Incredible."

"He's a numbers guy," Moran said, winking at F. Gregory. "Don't embarrass him. This is outside his purview."

"Shut up, Moran," Further snapped. "Why the hell are you even here?"

"Kenny said I could find a berth here."

"May I return to something Baconey mentioned?" Antony asked.

"Oh, now we got his TV show voice," Further said, laughing.

"What is it, Antony?" Freddie asked.

"In all the years I've known Kenny, he's not been looking for Eve. Because for him she was never missing."

Baconey nodded.

"Until when things started to change around here, he began to look for her."

"Lorna leaving him this place freaked him out some," Freddie said, pushing his chair back.

"Eve wasn't here," Baconey said in a low voice.

"Yeah, the house they had. Eve kind of created it. She's all over the place. Her hand. Everything has her in it."

Freddie's voice got lower and lower to a whisper.

"This place ain't her," Further said, nodding.

F. Gregory's voice surprised all.

"We have both sides of an equation to be solved," he said, poking at the table cloth with his fork. "The unknown is now known. Missing on one side and missing on the other. How does Kenny solve it? He goes in search. Not here. But where Eve is. Everyone missing is in the same place. It's where Eve is."

"And now he thinks Cissy is there to," Baconey said nodding.

"If all what you're saying here is what's going on with Kenny, he ain't looking for her in this world."

Further looked for some agreement here.

"Am I right here?"

"She's in this world don't worry about it," Moran said, reaching for more chicken parts. "I did a good job on this bird, didn't I? 425 until you smell it's done. Look, I found out earlier today Cissy got picked up for resisting arrest when they shut down the Public Defender Office."

"What? When were you going to tell us?" Freddie shouted. "Where the fuck did they take her?"

Moran shrugged.

"You were talking about Kenny. It was interesting. Look, the Mercs have been doing a kind of black op site removal kind of thing.

Where? Don't knock yourself out. They'll come to us. Her family."

"You are definitely not her family, Moran," Lucy told him.

"Hey, I'm helping here. They take them. Then you pay to get them back. It's like they freeze your computer and you fork over cash to get it released."

"Nobody's come around with that deal," Freddy said.

"Nobody comes around," Moran said, shaking his head. "It's in the mail. It's like you're paying a bill. Check or credit card."

"How do you know so much about this, Moran?" Further wanted to know.

"It happened to Klaus. Twice. I got the dunning letter."

"Did you pay? I bet you didn't pay, you shit."

It looked like Lucy was going to throw her knife at Moran. She didn't but F. Gregory did duck.

"No. I can't be extorted. It's not in my nature. Besides, I knew Klaus would get out of any black hole they put him in. He can get in and out of things like a cockroach."

They all thought about that and realized Moran was talking about himself. Then Antony asked if Kenny was getting any mail?

Freddy jumped up.

"If he's getting mail, he ain't reading it."

"Any more spuds?" Moran asked, lifting his patch up to look around the table.

"You're gone when Cissy comes back," Lucy told him, giving him a totally disgusted look. "So don't get too comfortable."

As Lucy Powell and F. Gregory lay on the porch rocker covered with one of the many colorful quilts Mrs. Hearder and Mrs. Woad had made and bestowed generously on friends, Lucy was wondering about F. Gregory's explanation as to why the Rev. Goodnow, long dead, was still broadcasting, randomly but always after midnight. These were not tapes he had made that were now being played. No, what he spoke about was stuff going on right then. He could have been a good mimic. Yes, it was Antony, Man of All Works! He slipped in an out of all kinds of voices."

"Antony has his own broadcast," F. Gregory said.

"And the TV show. Yeah. But what you're saying doesn't make sense. Tell me again what it is."

He laughed and drew the quilt up to their chins. It was Fall, closer to Winter judging by all the leaves gone. And it seems ever since he had helped in getting Cissie out of prison, Lucy had warmed to him. Like now. He didn't want to mess that up. Lucy wasn't easy to solve.

"It will be my F. Gregory side," he warned her.

"That's fine. Just don't go all quanic and stuff."

"I'll try to but none of this is certain. Hypothesizing. We can hear Rev. Goodnow because…and this is hypothetical -- he's in a time loop where space-time bends. And he's bent back to here. He's found the pathway."

"Whoa! So, he's here? That's how he knows what's going on? I mean where is he?"

She pulled forward out of the blanket.

"Hold on. When I said here, I didn't mean he's matter."

"What?"

"You and I are matter. This quilt is. The couch. Everything your eyes, which are matter, can see."

"And he's not that?"

"Hey, I'm not in my field here. There's no mathematics to it. Well, not any that connect. My mathematics doesn't make any of this real."

"He's invisible, right? He's going around town invisible. And listening. That's how come he knows what's going on."

He couldn't help laughing.

"He had to bandage his head like Claude Raney did in *The Invisible Man* so people could see him."

"You're making fun of me. You're so smart and I'm so stupid."

He put an arm around her shoulders.

"Believe me. You're gifted in extraordinary ways. Way beyond what I could ever learn."

"Really? You mean like Williams?"

He pulled her back so once again they were close.

"Well, there is a connect. Possibly. The matter that stars and planets and galaxies make up only one-sixth of the universe. The rest is invisible and we can't seem to reach but it has gravity the way matter does, enough to hold the visible universe together. But since we know little about this invisible part it may not be our gravity that keeps things together. Something else could be holding everything together."

He paused. He might have put her to sleep.

"Five sixths of the universe we know shit about."

"Well, we don't know enough…"

"To say what we know is right?"

"Sure, like a partial equation we can't solve but we go ahead anyway."

"And that's what Williams believes?" she said excitedly. "I mean he knows what the invisible glue is?"

"I guess that's what I was getting at. But ..."

"And he calls what's not matter Eve!"

"Does he? I thought she was a long lost love or something like that?"

"No, no," she cried out, punching his arm. "It's not a romance thing with him. He's got Earhart. No, Eve is mythical, mystical, visionary. Fucking astral! She's five sixths of the cosmos!"

"Ok," he said, in a rush to get out of the line of fire here because he knew when Lucy exploded like this, you had to get on the track she was on or get run over.

"I got the impression listening to him on that podcast of his . . ."

"It's a Q&A. He responds to questions but he doesn't give a lecture. I mean most of the time the questions are so dumb and infuriating that you never get to hear what's on his mind."

"True but I'd say he leans heavily on esoterica. When he's asked about Eve, he says she's the secret key to salvation. She has the light of salvation within herself. Esoteric stuff like that."

"No math, hun? Must drive you crazy. I saw one when they went all The Bible Says on him. The whole nine yards. Dissed God, opened up the box of sin, and got us all mortal when we were immortal. I kind of always liked Eve. I mean she was a perfect 10. And get this. Adam brings her to life?! I mean that was a one-off. Eve mothered the world. Am I wrong here? Who had the womb? Oh, wait. Jesus came from an immaculate womb. Keep the lady out of it."

"Baconey says Eve is just a lady who ditched Williams and he can't get over it. He's treating Williams for that. Love affair went traumatic bad."

"That's what happened to Baconey. He pushes that bit of trauma on all his patients. Wait. I thought the shrink talk was private? Did he ever say anything about me?"

"You went to him?"

"Fuck yeah! Him and forty others."

"Did they help?"

She hauled off on him with a pillow.

"No, the only help I needed was getting away from them. But I was a kid. Adolescent, Teenager. She's autistic. No, she's schizoid. No, she's just got border line personality disorder. No, she's dyslexic and dysfunctional. No, she's got OCD and ADHD. No, she's just a little bitch with a nasty personality."

"Who said that?"

"You did. At the prom."

"You mean after you hit me with a bottle?"

"You were being a dick. Do you think Williams is crazy?"

"He's got a kind of crazy, for sure."

"What's he looking for in the woods?"

As soon as she said it, she regretted it.

"I'm sorry. I didn't mean to bring that up."

"It's alright. I no longer think my Dad is lying somewhere out there crying for help. Williams thinks the woods are where the visible and the invisible cross. It's where Eve radiates, I guess. I've talked to him about it."

"You were thinking it would be a good place for your father to be? Even though he was murdered?"

He rubbed his forehead.

"Yeah, it doesn't sound like a good place. The woods. No Eve there."

"Well, these fucking Dizzyland tourists are fucking it up."

F. Gregory shook his head.

"Not anymore. I bought the woods."

PART FOUR

"For of the wise as of the fool there is no enduring remembrance, seeing that in the days to come all will have been long forgotten."
Ecclesiastes 2:16

"I thought everyone should know I'm defending Klaus Birke," Cissy said, as Baconey passed her the roast duck.

"I thought he was dead," Further said, pouring wine for himself.

"That's a rumor his son started," Antony told them. "He regrets not having killed his father long ago."

"He asked me to do it, in so many words," Baconey said, gesturing for the wine bottle. "He said I had the name for it."

"What's Klaus accused of?" Kenny wanted to know.

"He and his crew have been squatting in the *Founder Gasthaus*. They say it's legal because abandoned."

"It's not," Further said. "The place was full of paying guests. Klaus muscled everybody out."

"And the Street Thuggees arrested them? Those pricks."

"No, Lucy, those thugs quit. The Team wasn't paying them. The private predator declared bankruptcy and renamed. Their Hedge Fund cabal is facing felony indictments they're appealing. A Shoshone tribe owns the real estate the predators owned. That's going to the State Supreme Court but they won't take up the case. However, the real putsch is coming from Evangelical Pentecostals pushing for the End of Days. Anyway, it's a shirt storm. A couple of Techno fascists lenders who wear black shirts are in an AI fight as to who's going to decide what words mean."

"Is any of what you're saying true, Antony?" F. Gregory asked.

"Some of it is if from my own interviews, some from Earhart's reportage, a lot from what Faye's been hearing at *Sweeney's* but a lot of Russian bots may have worked their way in."

"It's all happening so fast I could cry," Lucy said.

"Is that all of it?" Kenny asked.

"Not exactly. If the Do What Thou Wilt party has its way, and Klaus and his pirates will want to get out of jail and go back to squatting *The Founder Gasthaus*, then you won't have to defend them, Cissie. But Birke's got a strong property rights following so squatting is a chop their heads off offense."

Stunning news someone said. Is there more duck? I think one duck per person would do.

"I'm leaning toward the property guys," Further said.

"Protecting the property you don't have, Further?" Lucy taunted.

"I like the Do What Thou Wilt clowns," Lucy said.

"They're pretty dangerous when you think that it is the nature of man to long after things forbidden."

"Do you have some man in mind?," Lucy demanded angrily. "F. Gregory is not like that. He doesn't long after things forbidden."

"No, I don't."

"That's because there are no forbidden numbers," Baconey said and laughed at his own wit

"Some sets of quantum numbers are forbidden," F. Gregory said.

"Jeez!" Lucy exclaimed. "Really, Frankie?"

Antony knew that having his *Casa Lorna* housemates on his TV show was a risk but as his days were numbered with that show, sponsors now mostly spending their money in cyberspace, AI and Crypto, he figured he should go out reckless, zany and explosive. He knew this chosen lot would do it for him.

He sat on an old rocker that JFK had used and on both sides of him sat the gang. He had told them to dress as they always did and they did except for Lucy Powell who was wearing her old Prom dress.

"Don't censor yourselves," Antony told them. "Respond to each other and don't look at the camera. Try not to talk over each other. Let people finish their sentences before attacking. But you don't have to piggy back supportively on what anyone says. Don't run a speech. Converse. Like at *Casa Lorna*. This is not a debate. Your zingers are not going viral. We don't want to hear your I Have A

Dream speech. You can be daft if it's witty. Okay, Here we go."

After his greets in which he introduced everyone and reminded everyone that there wasn't a script or a topic but certainly the rivalries in Founder after the collapse of the order of private predatory and venture raiders had left the gates open and barbarians, pirates, anarchists, magicians, gnostics, fascists and anti-fascists, spinmeisters, cryptologists, distributionists, singularitists, owners, laborers, nihilists, goths and visagoths and a fuck all lot were rushing in. The Sermon on the Mount and The Mishna were on their way to the Bog. The Golden Rule was a tattoo.

"Why is Moran here?" Further asked.

Moran, who was sitting next to him, said he was a *Casa Lorna* Emeritus.

"I invited him," Antony said, curtly. "I'm wondering why Birke is going around with a big dollar sign pin on this chest."

"Bog gold," F. Gregory said. "That mining has been shut down. The gold will stay where it's been for thousands of years."

"You know Birke has been trying to kill his father for that long. So far unsuccessful."

Baconey said that sadly. Enough to stopper the launch. Antony lit another match.

"What do you make of Birke's mantra: "Get the fuck out of my way!"

"I love it!" Further exclaimed, slapping his knee. "And his what does he call them? The Shitkickers?"

"You're an angry Greek," Baconey said, staring at Further.

"He's a wounded Achilles," Lucy Powells said, giggling.

"Go fuck yourselves," Further said.

"That was Rev. Goodnow's message to his flock," Antony told them solemnly.

"Really? I thought he was it's God's will if you get fucked over."

Antony saw that the AD was signaling danger. Probably the fucks. Antony laughed.

"No, Cissy, if you listened in a certain way to his sermons, you'll hear "Go now and go fuck yourself."

"And all I ever heard," Cissy returned, "was go now and serve the Lord."

"He always attracted a congregation of suckers," Antony said. "Rev. Goodnow never thought it was good now. Or after. He'd wake up, look around his bedroom and yell `Oh, shit!' or `Fuck me!' He was a nihilist. A total Void and Oblivion man. You die, you're swept into the Void with everyone else and you don't know who, when, what, where. It's a long Big Sleep you don't wake up from."

Antony saw he had stunned them and this lot wasn't easily stunned.

"Is there a Great Anesthesiologist then?" Lucy asked.

"I could use a whole lot more of that duck you made the other night," Further said. "What did you call it?"

"*Confit du Canard.* Duck cooked forever in its own fat."

"Now that's another kind of After-Life," Further said, happily.

Baconey had long ago diagnosed Further as a young angry disinherited Greek. Now he was the same but middle aged.

"I don't get what you're saying about Rev. Goodnow," Cissy said. "I mean if he was all like that about everything and everybody including God, why be a reverend in a church your whole life?"

"I would say he was hiding from a full realization that if there was no God, there was no morality and he had to pretend in a very dramatic way that there was so there would be."

"I think not, Baconey," Antony said. "He was a dark ironist. He wasn't running from what he knew. He made the church up. *Someday Eventual Holiness Apocalyptic Church.* Holiness was never now. His church deconstructed belief in there ever being a spiritual world for us. He mocked celestial belief."

"How do you know all this, Antony?" Cissy asked.

"A chatbot put it all together for me."

"Seriously?"

"Ok, there's two black folk in this town. Goodnow and me. We hung out together, don't you think?

"You're a black man, Antony?" Lucy said with a look of amazement on her face. "I never knew."

"Go fuck yourself."

"I personally think Birke is on to something."

"We know, Further. He has a need to kill his father."

"Yeah, that too. But, get the fuck out of his way? That's his mantra. That's the way some people get things done. For the good of everybody, right?"

"Really? Birke is a man who wants to eat up the whole world with you in it by the way."

"But why is what I'd want to know," Cissie had to ask.

"Not for the good of everybody certainly. He's a ME just ME and only ME self-centered bastard. You need to hit him with a crow bar and sink him in the bog. For all our good."

"He'd float right back up, Doc, and at it again. It's history."

"There's much in history we've put aside. Emperor divinities, feudal lords and serfs, black slave economies. . ."

"Not pirates," Lucy interrupted. "Klaus has a pirate crew. They're funny."

She laughed.

"They're squatting on property all over the town. And some of it has renters and owners living there."

"We'll go through a few more shootouts between Klaus and Birke, father and son and they'll kill each other."

"Naw," Moran said, speaking for the first time. "Birke can't get out of his own way. Nobody needs to kill him. Klaus? He doesn't want ownership of anything. He just wants to do what he wants and truth is, I partnered with that guy for years, he just wants someone to tell him what to do. It's what I did for him. I told him to be a pirate and have some fun."

"Why don't you tell him now to lock himself up," Further said.

Moran laughed.

"You don't want to rush to the ending when the show is still on."

"Am I wrong here, Moran, but for you everything falling apart around us …"

"They are not long, brother, the days of wine and roses," Moran interrupted, with a smile. "Better than the ending."

Antony could feel that ending going through his housemates.

Antony lit another match:

"I'm all for Johnny Williams," he said. "He's a cool calm walk in the woods."

"I'd ask Earhart about how cool that is," Cissie said. "She's the one been living with him. I'd say she does seem somewhat ambivalent about her Johnny."

"Walks in quiet woods," Antony said.

"Now that the tourists are gone," Lucy said. "Thanks to F. Gregory."

"Yeah, how did you pull that off, Frankie?" Further asked.

"17.8 million."

"Wow!"

"Frankie's sledge funds get over a 6% return," Lucy said proudly. "It's his mathematics."

"That's great return on 6%," Baconey said.

"60%," F. Gregory corrected him.

Further pointed at F. Gregory.

"I remember your father Frank thought you were kind of slow in the head."

"I didn't shoot or fish as well as Dad and Sheriff Jake."

"Yeah, those old bastards could hunt and fish. And Mike Woad too."

"Mike didn't hunt. He was a vegetarian. He lived on berries and fungi."

"Do you think he was killed or accidentally fell out of that tree?"

They all stared at Lucy who they knew was almost raised by Woad.

"Naw," Moran said, breaking the silence. "Here's the truth of it. Whose got bullets out in those woods? Hunters. Nobody was murdered. There was a shootout. There were no suspects because the suspects were the ones looking for the suspects. Jake and Frank have been accidentally shooting people in those woods for years."

"You're a lying son of a bitch, Moran!" Lucy screamed and rushed Moran, smacking him hard across the head.

F. Gregory jumped up and held her. Moran rubbed his head.

"She packs a wallop. Look, calm down. Jake and Frank were drunk. These guys barged into their camp probably looking to steal shit and they got themselves killed. Self-defense. Standing their ground."

"So why didn't Jake and Frank just say it was an attempted robbery? Why say they had to find the murderer?"

"I'm thinking that too, Doc," Further said.

They didn't notice F. Gregory was shaking until his chair started to move.

"Are you alright, Frankie?" Lucy said, her face still flushed with anger.

"No," he said. "No, it wasn't like that. Those murders happened long ago. When my grandpa would hunt those woods with Fatima, his lab. He heard her screaming. The girl they had in the tent. Two men. Fatima charged them. They shot her. And…and my grandpa got them both with his bird gun."

Antony suddenly felt that this show might pull sponsors.

"Go on, Frankie," Lucy said.

"So, that all opened up years later when I was camping with my Dad and Jake. All of a sudden, Fatima was there. And there were black lace panties hanging from a tree limb. They weren't there before. And when grandpa showed up there was a girl yelling in a tent that wasn't there before. Jake pulled me out of the campfire light and into dark bush and he told me that things were opening up and not to be scared and stay quiet. I don't know where my Dad was but I saw a man come out of the tent and yell at my grandpa and then a voice from the tent yelled for somebody to shoot. And then I saw my Dad yelling for Grandpa to get out of the way but he didn't and I was scared and tried to run to him but Jake held me back. They don't see your Dad Jake said but I could see that grandpa saw him because he pushed Dad to the ground and when the other man came out and fired a handgun, grandpa blasted him back into the tent where the woman was still screaming. Grandpa held his shotgun on the other man but he had his pistol out and he fired but grandpa shot him. And when Grandpa looked down at my Dad and then at me running over to my Dad, I saw he was bleeding and then it all closed up. And it was just Dad, Jake and me sitting by the fire. Nothing else. I looked for blood sign and there was none. Jake kept saying "It does open up strange in here" and my Dad told Jake not to say anything about this back in town."

F. Gregory hesitated.

"The murders Jake did always talk about perpetrated behind the *Founder Asylum* deep into the woods were long before. Long before any of us were alive. My Dad said Jake's brains got a bit addled by the experience. The two of them spent a lifetime looking in those woods. I don't know if things ever opened up for them again."

F. Gregory rubbed his eyes.

"It opens up in there. Time ago. In a space now. There in the woods. It addled me too. I couldn't come back. But now it's where I want to be. It was horrible what opened up. But I don't blame the woods. They are fossilized time. That's why I bought them. I don't blame the woods. No, I don't. I can't. They could open to Eve."

"Oh, my!" Antony said just as Sonny Bone rushed in.

"I'm late. Sorry. I got talking to Mike Woad."

"Where was that?" Lucy demanded.

"In the woods," Sonny said nervously. "Maybe."

"Johnny, where do you come from?"

"I stopped at *Sweeneys* to ..."

"No, not now. Before. Before you met me."

He got that look on his face that drew her to him but was also bloody annoying.

"I was looking for you."

"Well, you found me. But before that. When you were in *Founder's Asylum*?"

That clearly puzzled him.

"Before?"

"Amnesia? I mean you were in there because you didn't know who you were?"

"I don't think I was being treated for that."

"Well, tell me about your Mum and Dad then."

He obviously hit a blank.

"Perhaps you were left on a doorstep? And for some reason wound up at the Asylum."

A simple question had become ridiculously laughable. She was laughing. Wisely, she was recording.

"Does your birth certificate give us anything that might help here?" she asked. "For instance, where you were born?"

It took a while but they finally found the document.

"Yerevan, Armenia?" she read. "You're kidding? When did you become an American citizen?"

He went blank face again.

"This is incredible. I mean your name here is John Williams. Not very Armenian. I think your father was U.S Foreign Service working in Armenia. And … Show me your passport."

He pulled it out of the breast pocket in the worn double breasted he had taken to wearing.

"You carry it with you? Ok. Never mind."

She read that John Williams was born in NYC.

It dawned on her that there were probably thousands of John Williams and that this passport belonged to one of them but not to her John Williams. He was in the *Founder Asylum* because he was a pathological liar and he lied because he was delusional or he had multiple personalities each of which said different things about what anyone asked them. Like her.

"Why Armenia?" she said to herself but apparently out loud.

"Millions of years ago, it was where Eve was," he told her calmly as if he was reporting fact. Back to Eve, Earhart thought. It gets very, very tiresome with this guy. For the millionth time she thought about ending the relationship. It was a thought she never seemed able to act upon, as if the action was laughable.

"And for you, Johnny, she didn't die there."

That sentence upset him.

"There was no death in the Garden of Eden, so life could not be known. Eve brought life. She brought it to us."

"Okay," Earhart said, calmly, taking a quick look to see if her phone was recording. "I heard in my 2nd grade catechism class that Eve brought death into the world. So, you don't think that?"

"What would love be without knowing it could die or fade away or be troubled and angry?"

"A Hallmark card?" she said. "I'm sorry. The cliché lala you lay down gets my journalist skepticism going. So, you're saying in the paradise garden Adam and Eve couldn't really get it on, love each other because in that place death was kept out."

She listened to her own words.

"So, when she disobeys and bites the apple, she's getting to know and feel what love is? Otherwise, it's all same old/same old perfection. It's like you can't quench your thirst because you're always fully hydrated. I know that sucks as an example but it's all I've got right now."

"Eve comes to life in you. In every woman. But for me, it's you. There is no Founder but only a place where I can say I found her. You."

He had game with women no Romeo in any pickup bar in the world could match. He went astral.

"So, if we follow through on this, the Almighty creates the whole Eden drama to get death and fucking up into his creation because it's stuff perfection can't directly sanction. But, and this is the kicker, to get perfection he needs imperfection. Or she or whatever. Eve fulfills the Plan. Otherwise, Angels would have filled the bill for the Almighty. But they didn't."

Williams had retreated to his favorite spot on the sofa and was messing with his phone.

"Johnny, tell me if I'm crazy wrong here. Angels, whatever they are, are already here. There. Created. Why weren't they hired as dramatis personae to do what humans did?"

He didn't seem to be listening. She rephrased.

"Johnny, what do you think?"

"I think the angels being pure spiritual presences could not reveal what carnal matter is. Or death. Eve brought the two together."

"Carnal matter," she repeated. "The woods and the bog? And us?"

He nodded.

"We overhear the knowledge of Nature because we share the visible and invisible origin of being."

Ah, here was the opening.

"Johnny, don't you think that anyone who thinks he can do what you've just said is unusual?"

He didn't seem to hear.

"Maybe slightly unstable?"
Nothing
"Maybe just nuts?"

That evening, away from Johnny's stupefying take on things, she leaned toward thinking that she now knew why he had been in *Founder Asylum* and that he wasn't still in there because Baconey said he wasn't a danger to himself or others. A harmless lunatic. Who she had been living with for over a decade. She did love him, crazy or correct. It didn't matter. That's what love is, sung at all weddings. She could bracket out everything said about cosmogony and theogony, angels and edens, what you can overhear in the woods besides insect buzzing, birds screeching, and couples fucking didn't much matter to her. If Johnny, the delusional or correct, wanted to tie her to Eve, it worked for him and so fine. It worked for her. Who said love was reasonable?

A couple of days later and after the Celebration of Life for Gladys Farquarson who had died just short, as Faye Fata put it, of knowing who she was, Earhart was heavily into thinking about death, of losing Johnny, and thinking about what everyone in Founder she knew was thinking about: what happens after all the quarrels and dissensions in Founder blew up or equally possible blow away, no more than a vain striving after wind?

When she broached this confusion with Johnny, he told her that before and after are not before and after life but always already in life.

He said that with a smile as if, first, it made sense, and two, it would make her feel good.

"I don't think I'll ever know how to find you," she told him.

"Well, I'm here. The Sun warms the woods. The womb of Eve brings us into them."

"Did you just make that up?"

"I was talking with a generative Big Data fed transformer but it broke down."

"Well, it's been working to disastrous effect here in Founder. I heard the minutes of the weekly council and those members said that meeting had been cancelled. But the bots went ahead and held it. They gave out desire chips to new members. The new members were bots."

She paused. Johnny wasn't responding here.

"You heard of the *New Artificial Party*?" she asked, worn out by not knowing if he knew more than everybody or if he knew what everyone knew to stay alive. "It's running on a platform of the new normal is artificial life."

"I believe that's a bot report. That group doesn't actually exist."

She nodded. But what if bot existence was the new existence?

She didn't enter those weeds with him.

"So, how or why did your chatbot break off with you?"

"I don't know. I didn't relate anything I haven't with you. And you haven't broken off with me?"

"The first, I understand. You sent their artificial brains into a vicious suicide circle. The second, why I don't save my sanity and walk off, I don't understand. At all."

The *Floyd G. Wineapple Ballroom and Hippodrome Hall* could seat 564 and about that number, the town's total population, were now seated or being ushered to seats, when someone Earhart, seated up front, didn't recognize stepped up to the podium.

"Floyd G. Winepple, IV here. Gladys Farquarson was a forward looking woman. What she always looked forward to and hoped for was the prosperity of Founder. As a small business owner, she knew that the town must go forward and greet the future. She knew that computers would power the booming and energy-intensive artificial intelligence industry fiscalized by Crypt."

Just as Earhart couldn't believe what she was hearing, she heard a lot of noise coming from the rear of the *Great Hippodrome*. She turned as everyone did and saw a casket being wheeled down the aisle, Moran pushing from the rear, Lucy Powell and Frankie Jr on either side. They rolled the casket just below the podium and then Moran jumped up to it and pushing the speaker out of the way, pointed to the casket below and began to sing:

The stars above in Heaven are a-lookin' kindly down, The stars above in Heaven are a-lookin' kindly down, The stars above in Heaven are a-lookin' kindly down, On the body of our sweet Gladys friend

She's gone to be a soldier in the army of the Lord; She's gone to be a soldier in the army of the Lord; She's gone to be a soldier in the army of the Lord; Her soul goes marching on, our sweet Gladys friend

He stepped down from the podium and Klaus Birke, in full black mourning suit, took his place.

"Do what thou wilt!" he screamed. "And Gladys Farquarson did just that. She didn't follow the clock. She didn't follow orders. She made the menu. She never had a recipe. My shite blasted son, Leonard, wants to own all of us like property. I'm a sworn pirate and I have my crew right here in this shite blasted town and we'll board those ships of ownership and seize their cargo!! Not Christian, you say? We all should share on the socialist bread line? Or give up on our own brains and give them over to Whineapple the Fourth? It's a fucking artificial world we're building and we ain't in it. If you follow self-interest to make everything better in this town, it's fucked and so are you. Whineapple the Fourth is going to replace your sacred Self with one Quantum AI makes up. I wouldn't trust my life to what my crew of pirates judge to be in their own interests. Or trust you. It's not a human right to own property. It's not down there deep in human nature. Every pirate knows that what's down there deep in human nature doesn't have fuck all to do with human rights. No pirate fights for rights for all that started out totally fucked.

I'll end with a reading so please bow your head:
DO WHAT THOU WILT.
Because men that are free, well-born, well-bred, and conversant in honest companies, have naturally an instinct and spur that prompt them unto virtuous actions, and withdraws them from vice, which is called honour. Those same men, when by base subjection and constraint they are brought under and kept down, turn aside from that noble disposition, by which they formerly were inclined to virtue, to shake off and break that bond of servitude, wherein they are so tyrannously enslaved; for it is agreeable with the nature of man to long after things forbidden, and to desire what is denied us.

Gladys Farquarson broke the bonds of servitude and did what she wanted."

With this he plucked a three cornered pirate hat out of nowhere and put it on his head and stepped down from the podium.

Earhart wanted to ask Johnny what he made of that but he had his eyes closed and was snoring *sotto voce*.

She wasn't surprised when Leonard Birke followed Klaus at the podium. He was wearing a white suit.

"Don't worry about that guy. We're going to lock him up. He won't escape this time. You can pick your friends but you can't pick your Dad.

You notice he said little about our dear departed Gladys except a couple of lies. She hated him. She did. She told me that if Klaus showed up again in *Sweeney's* she'd call the mercenaries. He's a bad man. He's a very low form of humanity. I had him locked up in the Asylum for years. Padded Cell. Baconey let him out. He used his insanity test. To tell you the truth, I don't think that test works. You know he let Klaus out. I went along with it. He was my Dad. How long could I keep him in a padded cell?

But, believe me, if you don't believe what you heard just now, he's far gone, way far gone. He wants everyone to do whatever they want all the time anywhere.

Don't worry. We'll round up him and his pirates. You know what they are? They're low lives, criminals, rapists murderers, drug dealers, degenerates, losers, angry losers that couldn't hold on to anything you give them. They can't own. They don't have the intelligence. Or the drive and ambition. These I tell you are pirates without balls. They're paper bags you could go through with a fist.

But don't worry, we're going to put them away for a very long time. A very, very long time. We're gonna clean them up. Klaus is close to 80 or 90 so he doesn't have much time left. Poor guy. I mean I really feel sorry for him. But he was a miserable fucking Dad. But he's a danger. Has to go back in that padded cell with all the other lunatics. We'll round them up. Don't worry. And don't fool yourself that they don't want to own. They do. They want your property. They want it for themselves. Self-interest. And that's ok. That's how the economy grows. And, it has to grow.You know a lot of people have to die off if the economy stops growing. No body wants that.

And what's your self-interest? You want to grow. You want more than you have now. You didn't stop last year or ten years ago and say, well, I've got enough. I'm sustainable. If you want to be at subsistence levels, become a socialist. You want to give to the guy who doesn't work what you've got and you've got it because you worked for it? Go ahead. Fuck up your life. See who comes around to bail you out.

Here's the truth: when they can't cut it, like Klaus and his stupidos, they hate the game. They become the destroyers. They don't know how to grow. Really. It's beyond them. They're over their heads. So, they become haters. Clowns. Just a bunch of clowns. Do what thou wilt? They can't. They can't cut the mustard. And if they do what they want, maybe to make themselves happy, guess what? They get stopped. They get stopped by whatever you've got out there that's a rule, a law, a religion, a moral sense.

I don't wait for somebody to let me do something, I go ahead and do it and dare them to try and stop me. They're pretend pirates. They want to board ships and rape and pillage but they don't have the balls. Easily stopped and sent back to the asylum. I can't be stopped. And when I was in a Louie Asylum, I ran it.

Gladys Farquarson was like that. Like me. She lived her life to her own benefit. Prost!"

Earhart watched Leonard get down from the podium, her phone recording.

"So, they're both crazy. Father and son."

Williams opened his eyes.

"Is it over?" he asked. "What did they say?"

"So, the father…no, wait. Did you hear Whineapple?"

"Who?"

"Whineapple the Fourth. He said the town should let a secret tech company tear down the woods and build a 500 acre data center campus which will create a constant hum of generators behind guard towers with 24 hour security which will house thousands of computers that would power the booming and energy-intensive artificial intelligence industry. He said Gladys would like it."

"Sorry, I missed that."

"Wait. It gets better. Then Moran, Frankie, Jr and Lucy dragged in Gladys casket and Moran got up and led everyone in singing "John Brown's Body Is Lying in the Grave. He substituted Gladys name. Then Klaus Birke got up there and, let me see. If you're an owner, like of property or anything, he and his pirate crew are going to take that from you. If you worship self-interest, they are not your interests because AI is now yourself. You're artificial. Human rights and basic rights are as bad as ownership because who gave you those rights? Not the other creatures on the planet. And they started out fucked in the Bible. What's deep down in human nature isn't rights but some dark shit even his pirates don't want to look at. It's the nature of man to long after things forbidden, and to desire what is denied us. So, the solution is to have nothing forbidden and deny no desires. He ended by saying Gladys Farquarson broke the bonds of servitude and did what she wanted."

"Was that it?"

"No, his son Leonard, got up there and told us not to worry that his father would be back in a padded cell quickly. He said that a few times. They've never been able to hold him, have they?"

"Different constabulary have tried. But no."

"So, his father said that his son was also a liar because he stole property because he wanted it. But he couldn't do it legitimately because he couldn't cut it, the mustard, and Klaus and all his dirtbag crew were just losers and they would be rounded up soon. These pirates can't do what they want because they let rules and laws and commandments and regulations stop them but people with strong self-interest like himself don't wait for anyone to tell them what they can do and can't do. Self-interest is the only way to grow the economy because if it doesn't grow a lot of people will have to die off. You can't stop at a sustainable level one year because it's not sustainable the next. Ambition and drive, innovation and entrepreneurship keep pushing forward for more. And all that is now accelerated by AI and robotics. And paid for with crypt, a private currency. Then he said Gladys Farquarson was like that. Like him. She lived her life to her own benefit. Amen."

"I don't think Gladys would be enjoying any of this."

"Johnny, F. Gregory owns the woods, doesn't he? He said he bought them."

"He does. But there's a Private Predator firm and a Sillycone Valley investor who are making F. Gregory an offer through a broker. They'll hire a hundred or so AI IT people and provide STEM scholarships to *Rosa Parks Private Pre-School for Gentrified White Babies.*"

"I don't think this town has any AI IT people," Earhart whispered as Antony stepped up to the podium.

"I am Antony Obediah Abyssinian Nicodemus and I have known Gladys Farquarson for forty-two years. I am called a Man of All Work and I have worked off and on for Gladys at *Sweeney's Right Now Café* as waiter, bartender, bookkeeper beekeeper and bun baker. Paid positions. I am also a concierge at the *Founder Gasthaus* so you could say I've mingled with a variety of folk. Mike Woad once told me that wherever he went, there I was. Except up in a tree. As a sidle here I don't think Mike fell out of a tree. Other ways of breaking a neck. Maybe like F. Gregory says the whole world in front of Mike opened up and he went into it. I've had to keep both feet on the ground in my life so I add up things differently than that. Mike Woad was like the eyes and ears of those woods. He knew the routine of a chipmunk and the new nest of a robin. And so, I believe someone wanted to do something in those woods without being observed. And I don't think it was a bit of mating to propagate the species or squirrel hunting but something property like, as Leonard Birke would assume. What might be valuable in those woods that Mike Woad hadn't discovered? Or perhaps he had discovered something and was protecting it. I don't know. And it very well may be that with Mike out of the way, whatever was in those woods is now taken and gone.

Gladys and I pondered this many a time. I supposed what I'm saying is for her ear right now. It's still a mystery, dear Gladys.

There was no sign "Do What Thou Wilt" in any place my ancestors lived in this country. I learned from Rev. Goodnow that even men that are free, well-born, well-bred, and conversant in honest companies, do not have a natural instinct that spurs and prompts them unto virtuous actions, and withdraws them from vice, which is called honor. He was an After the Fall minister of God which means whatever natural instinct we have to be virtuous we left behind in that garden. Therefore, what's left could, grounded in a corrupted nature, want to do whatever the hell they felt like doing. They're not going to be rewarded in Heaven for that. Probably those pirates like Leonard Birke says will be rounded up and put in prison or the asylum, whatever privately owned facility has been contracted.

Leonard's been trying to put his Daddy, Klaus, back in a padded cell for a long time. Gladys and I had many a chuckle over this. Now Gladys was what we call a strong woman, tough and out spoken, which is what they say about women who talk and say about fellows with some color. We got along like that. But what Leonard believes is strength in plunging ahead and getting what you want and then more of it without allowing anyone or any constraint to get in your way, was not Gladys' strength. I am offended that he would connect Gladys to his "philosophy." And offended that Klaus would connect Gladys with his infantile rage. The man wants to break in and disrupt, to spit in his son's face. He's having a tantrum. That whole psychology should run the other way round."

He paused to take a drink of water. Earhart quickly looked at the flock behind her. Yeah, they were all goose necking the flock.

"Rev. Goodnow felt that there were marked and unmarked cards in the deck we're dealt. And, most significantly, the key cards were missing. That meant, to him, that you couldn't have belief at any point because that point was incomplete, could lead you astray, totally wrong. The blind man feels the elephant's tail and proclaims the elephant must be formed like a snake. Rev Goodnow didn't want to be pulled into that sucker's game. He felt that flying into life from some mystery and destined to fly out of that life into another mystery was not any kind of rock to stand on, or any kind of path to follow. The Creator didn't give up enough clues, or, in another formulation, too many that ran into each other.

Rev. Goodnow felt the safest and sanest and most rational path was to believe in nothing but the fact that he was living. Gladys was here with Rev. Goodnow but she did not have his anger at not knowing or being provided by a Creator with a path to knowing. If Jesus was man and Celestial, he was equipped to follow his own Beatitudes; but it was the man who was obviously crucified and the Beatitudes didn't work for him. They didn't keep the man alive. They can only keep the Celestial alive. Forever apparently. But we're not Celestial. Jesus in Rev. Goodnow's heterodox view was a one-off.

That was where Rev. Goodnow was but he didn't preach that. Gladys loved him. Gladys's strength was in feeling what Rev. Goodnow felt but she kept on loving too. She loved Sweeney forever. Loving beyond the love life offers us, the love of an After Life we cannot know, she had no interest in."

He paused and looked down at the casket.

"Did you, my dear friend?"

As he stepped down from the podium, there was the kind of eerie, numinous hush in the hall that no other speaker had produced.

On the way out, was Antony already magically there handing out *Celebration of Life* leaflets.

PART FIVE

Substances were thinned away into shadows, while everywhere shadows were deepened into substances:

"What's your name?"

"R.C."

"I'll be right over, R.C."

By half four, Woad was pulled up in front of *Town Global Propane*. He crouched down and peered under his van at the tank he had welded in place. It looked secure. But suspicious.

Inside the hangar like structure the office was vintage time-past. Propellers of paper on a couple of Army issue desks, farm calendars on the walls, black film noir phone, an old musket, overstuffed moth eaten critters, a buggy whip, an American flag on a wall looking like it had seen the farm, and a woman with a craggy face, heavy bags under her eyes and ropes of grey hair hanging to her shoulders, cigarette at the corner of her mouth.

"R.C. around?"

She looked up and squinted at him, smoke permanently closing one eye. She was doing a crossword puzzle.

"Out back. You can't miss him. Big with a beard. Also, he's the only one back there. Got a bark on him. Four letter word for no longer living?"

"Dead?"

"That'll do. Out back"

R.C. had a way about him. He wore a well-oiled onesie and had a smoke glued to his lower lip. Woad thought that was dangerous given the tanks of propane on the place. He mentioned his fear.

R.C. gave him a "What the hell do we have here?" look.

"Gotta go sometime," he told Woad. "Blown to bits go fast."

He then worked himself down to look under Woad's van.

"What the fuck all is this?" he said, pulling out from under and sprawling, one pant leg shoved into one engineer boot, down on the other.

"I think it will hold about 40 gallons," Woad told him.

"Didn't ask you that," R.C. snapped, working himself off the ground. Woad put out a hand but R.C. smacked it away.

"I asked you what the fuck is it? Never seen anything like it."

"It's a fuel tank."

"What's it fuel? The fucker is twitching. What you got in there, son?"

This wasn't going the way Woad had anticipated. The questions.

"It should be empty. I mean it stopped going and I figured it needed gas."

R.C. saw that this guy was more nervous than his usual who just came in for a drop off and grab.

"Mind telling me what it is that stopped going?"

Woad nodded nervously.

"Yeah, I think you're right. Probably something else. Sorry for the trouble."

Woad pulled out his keys.

"Hold on. We'll get you set up."

"Okay. What's it gonna cost?"

"Gotta check prices with Margaret for the odd tank fill up."

Back in the office, both Margaret's eyes looked closed.

She heard them.

"Not dead. Didn't fit. Gone fit."

"Sorry," Woad said, noting that the office looked somehow different, not cleaner but darker.

"He's got an alien. Forty gallons."

Margaret nodded, opened her middle desk drawer and pulled out a huge ledger that Bob Crutchitt or Bottleby or one of those shiveners might have used 200 years ago. Margaret turned the giant pages slowly.

"Used or new?"

"I'd say it's seen some light years," R.C told her.

"Got it. 82.75."

"Alright to give you a check?"

"Need proof," Margaret said. "No out of town checks. Unless, R.C. vouches for you."

"You that guy who lives in the woods behind the bog?"

Woad nodded.

"Don't know him. Heard about him."

Woad wrote out a check and then pulled out his wallet to show his driver's license. R.C. waved it aside.

"I know you."

Woad was confused. Strange but the strange was kind of familiar to him. He'd seen weird fungus eat Carpenter ants, geomagnetic fields to cause confused cows to kill themselves, squirrels fainting in the heat, racoons getting high on magic shrooms, foxes climbing through windows, bears out in the snow, chicks coming out of eggs.

"Hey, wait a minute," R.C. said. "Let me see that photo."

Woad handed over his license.

"Damn, don't ever make us look like we see ourselves."

"You need to practice your smile, R. C.," Margaret told him. "You need a good Selfie smile is what you need."

"Here, look at mine," R.C. said.

R.C.'s photo on his license looked like him in part with a flattened head probably wetted down but otherwise it looked like he might have looked under certain conditions but Woad wasn't sure what those might be.

"Show him that one when you were young and lively," Margaret told R.C.

R.C. did so and handed it to Woad.

It was a photo much fingered showing a young man smiling broadly. Woad couldn't see how as hard as he tried this young man had turned into R.C.

"Handsome," Woad said, handing back the photo.

"It's what's called a dareggyatype, "R. C. told him.

"Daguerreotype," Margaret said, correcting him. "13 letter word for a photo on a silver plated copper sheet."

She ducked her cigarette out on a pie plate sized ashtray and then lit another.

"Got any others?" R.C. asked him.

Woad took out a photo of himself and Earhart at the *Founder High School* Prom.

"She is fine looking lady. I bet you let her get away."

R.C. handed the photo to Margaret who squinted at it.

"Yeah, you'd look different now if she had stayed with you."

"Well, we were in high school then."

"Let me study that one some more," R. C. said and Margaret gave it back to him.

"For sure," he said, convinced of something.

"What?" Woad said. These two were unnerving him. Who the hell told him to come here?

"Well, she's got a look in her eyes of being right there," R. C. said. "And you look like you're from somewhere else but not there."

"What the fuck?" Woad exclaimed.

"Margaret?"

"I agree. You don't seem to belong there. Alien."

"I don't?"

"Well, you did wind up living in the trees, didn't you?"

Before Woad could answer, Margaret, getting up from her desk, which now had a lamp light shining on it, said:

"I'll make some java. Got time?"

And before Woad knew what he was saying said "Yeah."

In the back, surrounded by propane tanks, Margaret poured coffee from Mr. Coffee and the three sat down at a picnic table that had been dragged inside.

No one said anything and Woad wondered why he was there. Or still there. He was trying to think of the last place he had been but was coming up empty.

"I been up in one of them, you know," R. C. said.

"One what?"

"Alien spacecraft. They tend to hang around propane tanks like we got here. Refueling."

Woad thought about that. Not the alien spacecraft part.

"You can't use combustion for space travel," he said.

"Whatya use then, Mister Know It All?" R. C. thundered, slamming down his cup. Got a bark on him, Margaret had said.

"Where did they take you?"

"Cosmos. Took Margaret too one time. That's why she is the way she is now. Wasn't like that before. Before they took Margaret for a trip, she could keep an office clearer than a spit polished pair of them boots. And she could talk some too. Now she watches things fall apart and die."

Margaret lit another smoke.

"I don't suppose you saw how that alien spacecraft operated?"

"You gotta ask Margaret that one. You know, Margaret was a striking blonde before they whipped her up there? Had a face as smooth as a baby's butt."

R. C. reached out and patted Margaret's arm.

The three fell silent again.

"I saw one of those ships rising out of the bog."

Woad hesitated.

"I'm not sure what it was."

"Luminous?" R. C. asked.

"Spectral, I think. More of a presence than a ship."

He noticed that stuff around them was in shadows now.

"I'm talking stupid shit here," Woad said, running his hand through his hair.

"Ain't so," Margaret said.

Woad looked at her. She had the kind of look on her face that mothers have when they see their kids coming out of school.

It was then when he got up to finally go that he smelled the burnt and when he looked around all was charred, as after a mighty conflagration.

"Margaret got careless with her smokes," R. C. said. "Everything burnt to the ground. Propane will do that."

"And…and you escaped?"

R. C. boomed his laughter.

"No," Margaret said. "We got blown to smithereens."

Woad sat back down.

"Obv..obviously not," he told them, trying to smile, show them he could go along with a joke.

"Oh, we're dead, son," R. C. said. "And, if you don't mind my saying so, so are you."

Woad jumped up.

"Ok, I'm out of here."

"You shouldn't have told him that space ship crap," Margaret said.

"You didn't get whipped up into a UFO?"

Woad was beside himself in disbelief.

"We get visited for sure," R.C. said. "But not by saucers. A whole lot of stuff is around that you didn't see before when you're not dead."

"Like what?" Woad asked, in spite of not wanting to know.

"You got the feel of it, I think," R. C. said. "Otherwise, you wouldn't have rolled in here. You must have noticed living near that bog that some folks pop back up and some don't."

"They're not looking," Margaret said, nodding. "You got to be living like you know way beyond the having. Knowing way beyond what you think you know."

"You did that," R. C. told him.

"You mean my body is going to pop up at the bog?" Woad said, wanting to laugh.

"No, you came here instead," Margaret told him. "R. C. and me are kind of detectives. You fell out of that tree and broke your neck under very suspicious circumstances."

"Wait! You mean I was killed?"

"Don't get all worked up, son. Finding out who killed you ain't gonna make you alive again."

"So, what am I supposed to do?"

"Keep an eye out. Margaret and me figure that you'll make the killer nervous and he'll reveal himself. Or she. We'll be watching."

Woad felt "It's a lot" as people had taken to saying, along with "It's complicated."

"Is this it? I mean this the After Life? Aren't I supposed to be judged or something?'

"Margaret and me don't know anything about that. What's clear is you got to find who murdered you. After that? Damn, if I know."

Woad thought about this.

"So, it's kind of like I have a task?"

R. C. and Margaret nodded.

He studied them. They didn't look dead.

"And you…you and Margaret have a task?"

R. C. nodded.

"Sure do."

"We tell dead people that show up that they're dead."

"You go out of this garage, son, and you'll find yourself in your woods. Per usual."

After Woad wandered out, R. C. opined that Woad had taken the news well.

"And there was a grace about everything she did, laughed, walked, turned."

The first time Williams saw Earhart was at Sun Bone's annual *Black Swan Gala*.

It was a black tie affair and Sun had sent his tailor to deck out Willams and Moran properly. Now, the two of them stood close to opposite walls in the grand ballroom, Moran in his role as Sun's body guard surveilling back and forth the guests, and Williams looking now only at Earhart, although before he began this fascination, he had been looking at nothing.

"You do look very interesting," a woman in a black swan gown, said, suddenly by his side. "Sun said you were."

Williams turned his head to the left and down and looked at her.

"Thank you. Would you like to dance?"

"Oh, are we dancing? I didn't realize."

She looked at the silos of conversationalists posted throughout the ballroom.

"No one dancing? And no music? But there should be. Did you ever wonder why people chatter in tiny groups when they should be dancing?"

Williams' gaze had returned to Earhart.

"Do you know who that man is with her?"

"My dear, I know everyone. Of course, except you. Though I wish I were slightly less known. It's very difficult for someone like me to not draw attention in a small town. Now, if you identify the her, I can perhaps identify the him. Oh, we're done?"

Williams had suddenly walked with great purpose to Earhart and once there, he stood silently beside her. He stood there as minutes went by as if invisible until someone stopped talking or listening and looked at him. The others followed suit.

He ignored them and addressed himself to Earhart.

"Would you like to dance?"

While her friends exchanged wondering looks, Earhart said, amused:

"Maybe when there's music."

That reality seemed to jar him, judging by the look she saw on his face.

She looked at her escort.

"Is there something I should know here, Eddie? Is this the fellow you were telling me about?"

"I'm John Williams," Williams said. "Moran calls me Johnny."

"Yes," Dr. Oedipus Baconey, called Eddie only by Earhart, said to her.

The line of thought pursued before Williams' interruption began again the way a phonograph needle is put back on track.

"I think Eddie here knows you, Johnny."

"Eddie?"

"I call him that. How can I go around calling him Oedipus?. I'm Earhart Hearder. I write for the *Founder Chronicle*. I mean as long as it stays in print."

To this, Williams said nothing but kept his eyes glued on her. It was flattering but a bit unsettling she thought.

"Our readership is disappearing," she said. "Everyone is messaging within a small circle of like brains. Kind of tragic, don't you think?

""It's a tragic name," Williams said. "Oedipus."

"Okay," Earhart said slowly and then looked at Baconey.

"John doesn't recall faces," Baconey said, nervously, though he had no previous idea that this was a part of Williams' psychosis.

"Some are less in power and excellence," Williams said. "Some are more lovely and fair as Eve."

For some reason, Baconey thought that as a psychiatrist it was his duty to make the strange familiar especially in a social setting.

"Precisely," he said, smiling at Earhart reassuringly. "Nice seeing you, Williams."

He held a hand out to Earhart to sweep her away but she didn't want that.

"Can you get me a drink, Eddie?"

He hesitated and then nodded.

"But more favored by him who rules above," she quoted to Williams. "I wondered when I first read those lines in what way were angels more excellent than men?"

"Women are."

Baconey rushed back to them, skipping past partiers all looking in the same direction.

"Mike Woad showed up," Baconey said. "Uninvited."

When Williams looked, he saw Moran and Mike Woad inches from each other's face. Woad was laughing and Moran was stony faced.

"Moran has a Glock 19/30 semi-automatic," Williams said.

"Wow! Will he use it? Mike crashes this gig every year. He's not dangerous. He'll make a speech and then leave."

"Yes, he will," Williams said calmly looking at her. "Moran is far less than an angel."

They watched as the two tussled, Woad holding Moran's wrist keeping the Glock pointed to the ceiling and then dropping his left shoulder into Moran, he hefted him off the floor and then flung him against the wall. The Glock flew out of Moran's hand and Woad picked it up and fired it into the ceiling.

Woad turned to all the faces looking in shock.

"I came to say," he said, trying to catch his breath. "Every fucking one of these celebrations."

And then he screamed, "Eat the Rich!"

He was watched silently as he rushed out. He passed Sun Bone who was shaking his head.

"I knew getting a body guard was a stupid idea."

Sun went over to Moran who was getting himself sorted.

"You're fired."

"Amazing," Baconey said. "Incredible."

"Is that your professional response to that?" Earhart asked Baconey. "That display of human behavior? This is for the record."

Baconey looked at Williams and then at Earhart.

"I'll need some time," he stuttered. "They're both … I mean one lives outdoors ."

"Mike? Yes, he sleeps in trees. And the other was your patient? Like Johnny here?"

"Well, not quite the same. In fact, quite different. Dennis Moran and John Williams. Totally different diagnosis."

"Moran is an anarchist," Williams told them.

She smiled and touched his arm.

"I believe Mike is also. They should get along. No?"

"Let us fly and save our bacon."

He made to take hold of her hand and she moved back.

"What?"

"Do you want to leave?"

"Not right now," she said, looking at Baconey quizzically.

"I have to go," Willams said and started to walk away.

"Wait, Johnny. Can I come by to interview you?"

"Yes. I'll come to you."

He got out of there just as Kenny entered with his brother and the gang that followed Kenny everywhere when he was out and about. Sonny Bone and Lucy Powell was with them.

"They crash every year also," Earhart told Baconey. "They're the band. We could have danced."

She looked to where Williams had disappeared. He wasn't right. Not at all. But then he was very, very right.

"I see Williams made an impression."

"He's the type that impresses, isn't he? Is he on some anti-psychotics?"

"Not that I know of. I never put him on any. But you know Birke handed out anti-psychotics like candy."

Baconey could see she wasn't listening to him. One of the gifts he possessed as a mind analyst was his talent for sensing what was before the fact.

"I wonder if he knows how to dance?" Earhart mused.

"There's a Mr. Lucky wants to see you," Antony said, sticking his head in Earhart's office. "Only he ain't Mr. Lucky because I saw that movie and Cary Grant wasn't playing no screwball."

"Williams?" Earhart asked, pulling a comb and mirror out of her desk.

"One and, I hope for us all, the only."

"Send him up. And, Antony, don't go far."

"I got you. But I think this one is harmless."

They shook hands. He looked different out of the black tie but somehow better.

"I see you know Antony?"

"Yes, I do. He's the Man of All Work at the *Founder Gasthaus,* where I stay thanks to Mr. Bone."

"That's right. You're Sun Bone's new black swan. What's that all about?"

She had lined up her interview chairs in front of her desk. She sat in one and pointed to the other for him.

"He thinks I'm unusual. Swans are usually white."

"Are you? Unusual?"

"I like the way you turn your head and look at me."

She laughed. He was disconcerting. Was that unusual?

"And the way you laugh."

"Why, is it special?"

"If I were blind and deaf, I could still hear your laughter."

With that, she realized she hadn't gotten her phone recording going. Definitely recordable stuff. No article probably but memorable.

"But what is Bone looking for? I mean in you?"

"He thinks I can prepare him for what is non-existent."

"Such as? Give me an example. Like death? Spiritual preparation? Stock market crash? A winning horse? Appendicitis? Stage 4 cancer?"

She laughed. Self-consciously now.

He had an awful habit of staring.

"I wonder if what I'm feeling for you now was non-existent but always existing and I didn't see you."

She wondered if Antony was really nearby though once again the way he flattered her had no danger to it.

"Or if it never existed and you made it so."

She laughed and it was a nervous laugh. That couldn't have sounded good.

"You've got quite a game. Why are you putting this rush on me, Johnny?"

She immediately regretted going familiar like that. Was this an interview for an article or a what?

She got up, went to her desk and pulled out a pack of cigarettes.

"I gave these up. Not really. They're bad for me. The smoke will be bad for you. I'm not good if I light one up? Really, I'm not good. For you."

She lit her cigarette. Ok. This guy is unusual in that he totally confuses, angers, mystifies and attracts you. He does it all at once. She blew smoke in his direction. He sat as calm as ever. Antony had to rush in, not when he heard her screaming but when it went silent for too long.

"Interview over," she said, going to the door and opening it. Antony was seated on top of a nearby desk.

Williams got up and followed her to the door. She didn't turn to look at him.

"If you get a chance, could you message me on what you think is any good going on over there at *Founder Asylum*? Also, what you've done since hired for Sun Bone? And, leave any observations about me out of it. Ok?"

Before he could say anything, she closed the door on him.

She thought of speaking to Eddie about Williams and exactly what was wrong with him but the thought of finding out convinced her that it was easier not to see him again, not to have anything to do with him.

So, when she found Johnny sitting in the sun on the *Founder Asylum* veranda sharing a lunch with her mother and Mrs. Woad, she wasn't surprised. There was destiny at work here. The more you hung around with the irrational, the more you believed in destiny.

"Oh, E!" her mother called out when she saw her. "Come listen to what Mr. Williams was telling us about being mindless isn't any help at all."

"That sounds…right," she said, kissing her mother and then Mrs. Woad. She nodded to Williams who had stood up.

"You're in time for lunch, dear. Antony!"

Antony was already there pushing a chair for Earhart.

"Thank you, Antony," Earhart said, looking quizzically at Antony. "Didn't I see you at the office this morning?"

"Oh, my! It was busy, wasn't it?"

"I'll have my usual BLT, Antony," Mrs. Woad said.

"Is it, dear?" her friend said. "Your usual?"

"Of course, dear. Buttered lemon trout. The French call it something French."

"I'll have the same, Antony. E?"

"I won't eat. I can't stay long."

"Nonsense. She'll have the same. BLT. Mr. Williams? I bet you don't eat meat?"

"When?" Williams said, and Earhart rolled her eyes. Here we go again.

"Why, when you're a Yogi."

"He's a Guru, dear."

"Fascinating," Mrs. Hearder replied to her dear friend.

"What do you think Mr. Williams is, dear?" Mrs. Woad asked Earhart.

She almost laughed, looking at the expression on Johnny's face. He was a wonderful amusement.

"Well, I don't think he's at all about Eastern tranquility of mind. To…to find your spiritual self."

"Oh, is that true, Mr. Williams?" her mother asked Williams who was looking down at the BLTs Antony had put on the table.

"Mr. Williams …"

"Can I be Johnny to you?'

She took a deep breath.

"Johnny, I believe doesn't want to neutralize his mind. I believe he just wants to see things clearly. As they are without ignoring conditions and facts."

"Earhart is a reporter of facts, Mr. Williams," Mrs. Woad said. "Johnny."

Johnny picked up a sliced half of his BLT and stared at it.

"There is something in us that can overhear all things in this world we are not," he said solemnly.

"Oh, that sounds so much like a Yoga!" Mrs. Woad exclaimed. "I think my son agrees with you. He lives in the woods overhearing. He hears herbs."

Earhart wanted to say Mike ate them too. So, he could overhear.

"There's a knowledge not just in the stars," Johnny said then bit into his sandwich.

"But that's all the astrologists report," Mrs. Hearder said. "What the stars say."

"What did they say today, dear?"

"Pluto is ascendant. I need fundamental change."

"Where might this knowledge that an oak leaf has come from, Johnny?" Earhart asked, set on pushing this lunatic hard.

"Not everything has a form," Johnny told her, naïve as to her intent. "Something becomes facts and conditions and something doesn't. The world is not made from nothing. It's like a fish pulled from the sea. We're tied to the whole. All things material are also astral. And the way whatever has not the human mind still has its own way of knowing the astral. It could not be otherwise because we swim in the same waters from which we emerge. It makes no sense to silence our minds of that affinity."

"Oh, my! That is the craziest shit ever I heard in this place where folks naturally talk crazy."

Earhart looked at Antony who was standing behind the table with a towel on one arm.

"Quit the yowzah, Antony. Did you get that on your phone."

"I got it going anytime Williams show up."

"I think that was magnificent, Johnny," Mrs. Hearder exclaimed. "But I'm not sure I got the gist of it."

"Why Johnny means that Susie. You know my dear Susie."

"Your Siamese

"Yes. Departed. But I knew that Susie knew a great deal but was holding back. She had a passive egregious personality."

"I do remember that, dear. But she was affectionate."

Earhart closed her eyes. When she opened them, there was Johnny looking at her like he had found heaven. Which was her. She wanted to vomit instead she said

"Want to go for a drink, Johnny. I need a double of anything on the rocks."

On the way to *Sweeney's* she asked him if booze ever spoke to him.

To romanticize the world is to make us aware of the magic, mystery and wonder of the world; it is to educate the senses to see the ordinary as extraordinary, the familiar as strange, the mundane as sacred, the finite as

It was also a Founder tradition to have one Mayoral debate held at *Sweeney's Right Now Café*. Gladys said it had been started In the Ur-Sweeney days when the Café, said to be the oldest on the planet, was called simply *Founder's Place*.

Although Williams was not running for office, though she had heard talk of he being urged to do so, which totally amazed her, as she entered the café as a reporter of the debate, she saw Johnny at the bar barstooled between two known town floozies. She could see that his eyes went to her like a razor sharp beam as soon as she entered but she did her best to cut him on her way to what she called her cat bird seat against a wall to the right of the carved out debate stage.

Faye was waitressing, Further was tending bar and Antony, Man of All Work, was to ask the debate questions. She was sure he would do so in Oxbridge tones. Why he mimicked speech styles annoyed her but amused him. "I goes from Southern cotton picker to Prof Higgins" he had told her.

"He's a big favorite in here."

Gladys was there at her elbow.

"Who?"

"The guy you're doing your best to ignore."

"Obvious?" Earhart said and laughed. "He comes in here a lot, doesn't he?"

"We got his slippers under the bar."

They both laughed.

"Tell me, Gladys, off the record. What's with him?"

"He's a drunk. Just kidding. Types in here. Coffee clutches, heavy drinkers, retired geezers, romeos, amnesiacs."

She paused and lit a cigarette.

"And then there's Williams. He's like Jesus showed up at a bar. Christians ain't gonna say that."

Earhart glanced at Williams and sure enough he was looking at her.

"I don't see him like that."

"Yeah, I don't either. He's more like that guy who drops down in a saucer comes out with a twenty foot high robot and stares at people. What was the name of that flick? *The Day Things Went Stiff*?"

Earhart didn't respond and then said she didn't know that one.

She noticed Kenny and Freddie and their posse coming in and grabbing some booths. Then Lucy Powell and F. Gregory who went to the bar. For the first time she saw Mike Woad sitting there. He came out of the woods and into town on rare occasions. He was a skillful hunter gatherer and swung through the woods like Tarzan, though she didn't accept that as fact. All he did when they were in high school together was throw a football.

"What's Moran doing standing over there?" Earhart asked.

"Security. I felt sorry for him after Sun Bone tossed him."

They both stared at Moran who was back to wearing his pirate ensemble.

"I don't know about that guy," Gladys said, blowing smoke away from them.

"In the same way as with Johnny?"

"Oh, Johnny?"

"I interviewed him for an article. We didn't get engaged. Absolutely no plans to marry. How's he different?"

"From Moran? Mostly, he's not. They both belong back in *Founder Asylum* but our shrink who couldn't tell who belongs in there and who doesn't let them out. But I'd say Moran is a bullet in a gun and your Johnny is an empty chamber. I don't mean dumb, I mean hard to see what he is."

Before Earhart could respond, Antony was at one of the standing mics doing his Oxbridge.

"In this corner, weighing. Wait. Wrong venue. Welcome to the 659th *Sweeney Right Now Café's* Mayoral Debate. I'm ..."

"We know who you are Antony," someone shouted.

"For those who don't, I'm Antony Emancipated Nicodemus. The questions I will ask the candidates were prepared and sealed until now by *Global Community Private Predatory* and an Unnamed Panamanian Offshore Account. We welcome the candidates Sonny Bone..."

Kenny's crew gave out some ball park yells.

"And an illustrious descendant of The Founder, Tina Firewoad."

Tina was greeted with silence and grunts and throat clearing.

They were many minutes into the debate when Johnny came over to her.

"May I sit?"

She nodded.

"You smell of floozie," she wanted to say but didn't. She wondered what a newly released mental inmate's sex life was like. And why was she referring to an ex-Nun and a school librarian as floozies? Jealousy. And it's necessary: love.

"Fire and Sun," Williams said.

She looked at him quizzically. Here we go again. He didn't disappoint

"The Sun is the landline to Angels. Fire is the power to do so."

"And so, in this debate, who wins?"

He smiled at her.

"That's ancient myth. This is reality."

Surprise. Surprise.

"So, you don't believe in angels? Not even overhear them?"

"I see enough in front of me. I don't need imagine more."

She woke up to the booing.

Tina Firewoad was ignoring it.

"My opponent here wants to re-distribute the wealth. Maybe. He's maybe about everything. He's not fired up about anything. I am. Instead of piecing out the little we have to everybody, let's give all our support to those who have proven they can take a dime and make a dollar out of it, those who can take an empty lot and build houses and businesses, those who have gone to the best schools and know what needs to be done. Look, you can all wait around the campfire, freeze, and starve or put whatever you have left, the one horse, to one person who can get through, find a way out, and then return with more than you'd ever have if you share, redistribute. You all die together or you get behind the achievers and enjoy what they harvest. Thank you."

"You didn't take notes," he said to her.

"What? No. But I'm recording."

Gladys was with them now.

"She won't win. This town doesn't know her."

"Not an old family here?"

"Yeah, maybe a hundred fifty years ago. They went off and made fortunes anywhere fortunes could be made."

"And why is she back?"

"She really isn't. She's a front. If she wins, she'll be taking orders from some Russian oligarch."

"How do you know this, Gladys?"

"I overheard it," she said, winking at Williams.

Smartass, Earhart whispered to Gladys, both smiling.

Antony was throwing a question at Sonny Bone, who now stood, twitching and making sucking in nostril sounds and facial convulsions. He had a two-toned Club jacket on with the LamB insignia.

"Is it true, Mr. Bone, that as Mayor you will make an effort to re-distribute the wealth?"

"Who said that? I mean maybe."

"Your opponent, Ms. Tina Firewoad said you would. Maybe."

"I think I said that in reference to a possibility of…of something that might happen. Possibly."

"You know, Mr. Bone, that you are not on a witness stand and I am not cross examining for the prosecution. So, you can tell voters who maybe might vote for you what you mean by what you've just said."

"I love the way Antony puts on that Brit hi-tone," Gladys whispered to Earhart.

"Not a put on. He was born in London. Went to Oxford."

"No kidding?"

Sonny was mumbling toward saying something.

"What if somebody with a whole lot of money dies."

Antony waited.

"And?"

"And and he can try to make more and more money."

"While or after or before he's dead?"

"Both. Maybe."

"Go on."

"Should he do that or should he do the other thing."

"And by other thing you mean?"

"Re-exhibit the money. Maybe."

"I see. Re-exhibit the money. To who?"

"To his son. To me. Maybe."

The giggling and the chuckling had now kicked up to loud expressions of amusement.

"And do you need to become the Mayor of Founder for that to happen?"

"Maybe."

Tina Firewoad had turned in her seat and was looking at those around her, her eyes wide in disbelief but tearing in amusement.

"I don't care if he's an idiot," Gladys said out loud. "I'm not voting for that stuck up bitch."

With a continued seriousness, Antony asked:

"So, you wouldn't call yourself a Socialist? You're not running for mayor as a Socialist? This is not a maybe question. It's a yes or no."

"Yes."

"So, you're on a Socialist ticket?"

"Maybe."

Booming laughter.

"At least we'll have some fun if he's mayor."

"Do you have a problem with the wealthy, Mr. Bone?"

"I just think that somebody who makes a lot of money in Founder and goes off with that money and loses it someplace else, then I think that's like a drainage we should stop."

"And as mayor how do you propose to do that? I mean violate the Fifth and Fourteenth Amendments to *The U.S. Constitution*?"

Sonny had a dumbfounded look on his face.

"You can't take someone's money or property without due process or compensation," Antony explained.

"Maybe you can take it if they want to leave with it without being fair to …to others who were…were there."

"You mean there as in the scene of a crime?"

"Maybe."

"Mr. Bone, don't you think you'd be better off running for mayor in, say, a city in China?"

That ruffled Sonny's Club jacket.

"We're not Chinese. We just got inherited eyelid issues. Our first name was Boneset. Like the tea."

"Would you like to make a concluding appeal to the voters?"

Sonny shrugged his shoulders, shuffled his feet and looking over at Kenny and his crew who responded with a thumb's up said:

"I think we should keep the woods, the bog and the money."

He paused.

"Maybe. Thank you for voting for me and not for her."

"Amazing," Gladys said. "Well, got to work. People will want to drink after that."

Antony shook hands with the candidates and then headed for the kitchen where he was making the Debate Day special, Red, White, and Blue Beans and Rice.

Earhart didn't know when it had happened but Williams's hand was holding hers. She wasn't surprised then when he walked her home. She wasn't surprised when he stopped at her door, her back to him and she knew if she didn't go in but turned, this very strange man, this Johnny Williams, would be hers and she'd be his. For how long? Reasoning anything was now far beyond its range. She turned to him, absolutely reckless, unknown destiny.

There were more than a few things troubling Frankie, Jr's mind that June as he stared at his face in the bathroom mirror.

"Ok, Crime Fighter, lay it on me," the scowling face reflected now in the mirror asked him. "You're scared to take Lucy Powell to the Prom because one: she'll go full bezerkazoid at some point, two: you'll try to calm her down but she don't calm, three: the Varsity Big Men on campus mock you and her; four: you won't take it but you do because, like they say, you're Lucy's little boy toy, and then five: Lucy starts banging the shite out of the VBM's with Freddie Rama's bass and the cops arrive. End of scene."

Frankie, Jr thought about that. Well, he must have been because he was the one talking in the mirror. Yeah, it was a big fear but that wasn't it he told himself. He didn't fear Lucy's bi-polarity as Dr. Baconey had explained it to her grandfather, Harry Powell, who had explained it to Sheriff Jake Wilcox. "So, let's not be pulling her in for every misdemeanor infraction, right?" and Jake nodded he wouldn't. From Jake it went to his long- time hunting buddy, Frank Coletti who had sat down and explained the situation to Frankie Jr.

"Remember that movie *Ten Faces of Eve*" Frank asked as he, Frankie Jr and Sherrif Jake Wilcox sat around a camp fire after a long day of almost spotting a couple of Spikes.

Frankie, Jr. shook his head.

"You see, in that movie, Eve has a lot of other Eve's inside her and they all have different personalities."

He paused and looked to Jake.

"Like all the different personalities in Founder were crammed into just one person's head."

"Exactly. So, that's Eve's deal. Follow?"

Frankie Jr nodded.

"Eve is Lucy?"

"No, no, no. Lucy's only got two Lucys going on."

"I seen them both," Jake said. "One's hell fire doozie and the other is a sweet pea."

"But Jake loves them both. Right, Jake?"

"Treat them both the same. Love wise. It ain't her fault her Daddy turned up dead right in these woods when she was squirrel small."

"Why was he dead?" Frankie, Jr. asked.

"Two bullets straight to the frontal lobe," Jake said. "Ruled out suicide. It was a professional hit."

"Jake and me think that it was a kind of warning to Harry Powell, who was Mayor at the time."

"What was he being warned of?"

"Don't know. Either Harry backed off and they got what they wanted," Frank said.

"Or he didn't. and Harry got to them before they got to him."

"Like they did his son."

"Lucy's dad."

Frankie Jr was trying to remember the name of the movie he had seen with his Dad and Jake that had the same plot just told.

"All to say," Frank said, smiling at his son, "if Lucy split into two, she had her reasons."

Frankie, Jr. thought it best at that time not to bring up asking Lucy to the Prom.

Somehow both his mother and his new step-Dad found out about that and it didn't take much time for them to corner him in Step-Dad's home office to bring up their concerns. Step-Dad sat behind the desk that had been a legacy to him from his father who had gotten it from his father. And so on. So, the desk was very old but everything on it was arranged. It was like if things knew their place and when they might be out of it. In his mind he referred to the man who his mother had found after she left Frank Sr. or, as Jake told it, had found him before which led to the divorce, Sir. Frankie, Jr. remained a Coletti. When asked by the judge Frankie Jr had declared that he was Frankie Coletti, Jr. He couldn't think how worlds could collide to change the nature of that. He called Step-Dad, Sir and not Step-Dad because he hadn't been adopted. He was old enough to say no to that. Frankie, Sr was the best father a kid could have. And it was Frankie Jr's thinking that he was probably the best husband any woman could have.

Now, seated in a chair across from his mother, both of them in front of Step-Dad seated behind his desk, truth was Frankie Jr. didn't like either as much as he liked Frank, Sr and Sheriff Jake Wilcox. The idea of marrying Lucy Powell was as remote as Alpha Centauri but he did wonder what it might be that kept a wife, if he married her, loving him or deciding to go off and find a Step-Dad.

'Her mother is in a sanitarium," his mother told him.

"No chance of parole is what I heard," Step-Dad said.

"I didn't know," Frankie, Jr said, after a few minutes sitting there as they stared at him.

"You're dressing more and more like that Mike Woad living in trees. Can't you wear any of the clothes I've bought you?"

"It was never proved but the mother was most likely the one who shot Powell."

"Twice in the head," his mother affirmed.

"The message here is clear," Step-Dad said. "The apple doesn't fall far from the tree."

"And in this case the apple, dear, is poisoned."

"Baconey said she has permanent schizophrenia. She goes from Dr. Jekyll to Mr. Hyde."

Step-Dad loved to use literary references as he was the 10th grade English teacher at *Fountain High* and would be, as Frankie Jr, knew, one of the faculty chaperones at the Prom. Frankie Jr had never been in any of his classes but friends who had told him he was a tool on wheels.

"And back again," his mother affirmed.

"It's just one thing," Frankie, Jr. said weakly. "The Prom. I probably won't ever see her again."

"Excellent!" the Tool exclaimed.

"You could ask a girl who has some control of herself," his mother said. "You can't really like someone who might at any moment change into someone who frightens you."

"It's come up more than once at faculty meetings as to why Lucy Powell is with us and not in a controlled environment. She's frightened more than a few of her classmates."

"She doesn't frighten me," Frankie Jr. piped up. "I like her. I think I more than like her."

The Tool, for that was how Frankie Jr was now calling Step-Dad in his mind, and his mother exchanged meaningful looks.

"Well, when someone thinks he loves someone when he's in high school..."

"I'm graduating."

"He will find those thoughts vanish very quickly and he will move on to maturity."

You'll be in a whole new world at MIT. Wonderful smart fellow students."

"And sane," The Tool said.

This wasn't the first time Frankie Jr regretted his scholarship to MIT. He didn't want to leave Founder.

"You know, F. Gregory, I'm surprised a young man gifted in the Higher Mathematics is even going to the Prom."

Frankie Jr shot a cold stare at The Tool. He hated to be called F.

Gregory. And he hated anyone to assume because he liked mathematics that he had no feelings, could not have a crush on someone so lovely and lively as Lucy Powell.

And then the last troublesome matter he saw that morning as he looked at his face in the mirror was Lucy herself.

First off, she hadn't exactly said she'd go with him. Secondly, she called him F. Gregory in a taunting way as if had done what Frank Sr had feared: become a tool like The Tool, that he had no fight in him, that he wanted to rise up out of Founder and all its superstitious rot and nonsense. He didn't know where she got that but he knew she read a lot. She read so much so far away from what fascinated him. The huge book she said was Rabelais or the tiny one she said was a Yale Shakespeare while his bedtime reading was so very different. Such difference would not generate compatibility was a thought he had but he also had the thought that mathematics had no answers here. He couldn't pick up his Shakespeare as she sang out to him one day. She had a sweet voice. Whether both Lucies did he didn't know. *The Housekeeper and the Professor. Uncle Petros and Goldbach's Conjecture. Number: the Language of Science. A Tour of the Calculus. One, Two, Three: Infinity.* He would rattle these titles off as if they were engaged in a wild battle of the books. It was clear to him in every encounter with Lucy that she thought he was a dunce with no back bone, that he would never measure up to his father or Sheriff Jake or Mike Woad, nor would Kenny and Freddie let him join their gang of total coolness. In her mind, numbers didn't say what she wanted to hear from a boy. He knew that but he didn't know how he knew that and so whether it was true or not. But then, this other Lucy, would say something like he was as handsome as his father, Italian blood of dark and handsome, bedroom eyes. She actually said that to him. Or, one of her, did. Or, you're tall, why aren't you playing varsity? Or, sometimes she would recite to him as if he were Romeo and she Juliet. It inspired him to find the play and read it. It left him thinking it would be better to watch the movie, which put him to sleep.

He left off with his mirror self-thinking that he could only hope that when he went to pick her up on Prom night she'd be there and the she that was there was the one who thought he was tall, dark, handsome with bedroom eyes.

"Hey, bro, we got two more songs on our playlist and that's it."
Kenny, who was fiddling with his amp, just said OK.

"And we're playing till 1AM."

"OK. I don't think you put this amp back together right."

"Antony was on that."

Kenny stood up.

"It'll do."

"What?" Freddie said, tensing up with their predicament. This was their first gig that wasn't in somebody's basement. *Founder High* gym. The wholesome student body.

"The amp," Kenny said, hefting his shoulders in his vintage Goodwill sport coat that had threads of yellow running through the marble blue. "Antony can stretch the fills."

"What say?" Antony called from stage pulling out his sticks.

"You got say three or four to fill a set?" Kenny asked, climbing up to him.

Antony laughed.

"I knew you boys was amateurs."

"We ain't amateurs," Freddy shot back. "We just got more time to play and …"

"And no songs. Yeah. Amateurs."

"You got a couple?" Kenny asked. "You got that Lil Richard goes ten at least."

"Yeah, I got that. But you see that blonde girl down there?"

He pointed.

"I see a lot of them," Kenny said.

"Name's Eve. She got a voice on her."

"No way, man" Freddie said, shaking his head. "We never heard her. She could be a frog."

"I'll go talk to her," Kenny said, hustling his shoulders and his balls and getting down from the stage.

"Can we go to the movies just once without your band sitting behind us?"

"The crew? You forgot your glasses, didn't you?" Kenny asked Eve.

"No, I didn't. Did the movie start? No. So?"

"I think you look good with your glasses on. Sort of like Lois Lane."

"I thought you didn't want any popcorn? Lois Lane? You mean Superman?"

"That's the duo."

"He had glasses. As Clark Kent. She didn't. Could you tell whoever of your crew kicking my seat if he doesn't stop I'll kill him."

Kenny turned and told a row of guys to go seat a few rows back.

Half way down the movie someone screamed like Tarzan from up in the balcony of the *Founder Fortway*.

"Woad," Kenny said, not turning around. "He loves these Tarzan movies."

"He's not right, you know."

"Probably. He's a good guide through the wood lot."

"Not for me. Besides, Nickels, *Gidget Goes to the Beach* is not a Tarzan movie."

"You think Pancakes will grow up to like Rhodies as much as we do?" Kenny asked Eve as they both did some weeding around the plants in late Spring.

"I didn't grow up to like what my parents made a big fuss over."

"Like what?"

"Like getting married to you"

And then she whacked him with her trowel.

"They didn't like me."

"I think they didn't like your friends more than they disliked you."

"What? Freddie?"

"He's your brother. But they did like him better."

"Antony? Who's a better guy than that guy?"

"He's a whole different category. But Sonny? And Mike? And what's his face?"

"Leonard? He's got issues. His Dad is in prison."

"You know, if you went to prison for a long time, you'd never see Pancakes grow up."

"What? That's goofy. See, these babies, water them deep once a week the first season and then let Nature take care of them. Of course, these babies do look a bit unnatural. I mean their size and colors and all. Amazonian. Woad says the human touch ain't that big in Nature's opine."

"Mike Woad speaks for Nature?"

"Nobody to stop him."

"Well, the Asylum staff could net him on the streets."

Kenny laughed.

"That's why he stays in the woods. He says it's all speaking to him all the time."

"So why is it deadly silence when you and I take walks in there?"

"You're too lovely for them. It's awe. Shuts the plants up."

She hit him again with her trowel.

"This is an English roseum rhodie," Kenny said, getting up and pointing to the rhododendron "She blooms with big pink flowers that cut into the leaf. I mean it's an effect. Kind of goofy though the way it blooms different every year."

"You think, Nickels, maybe that's why it doesn't die?"

"Whatya mean?"

"That she's always the same yet always different. Like the seasons."

"If you tell me why you've been calling me Nickels from the first time we met, I'll tell you why some of everything doesn't die."

She laughed.

"It's my mystery," she told him. "I don't have to explain."

Every time she told him she liked being a mystery to him, she'd laugh and he'd get more annoyed.

"What season do I remind you of?"

She had that teasing look in her telling him she knew he didn't know. But nevertheless, he said:

"All of them."

A ferocious, dark early February snowstorm, not nighttime but in midday, when the whiteness of the swirling snow, as well as the mounds of snow quickly building from the woods edge to the bog and down main street passed the *Founder Gasthus* and passed *Sweeney's Right Now Café* and City Council and *Founders Fortway* and the *Founders Private Library*, a torrent of whiteness in air, water and earth and yet the landscape and the townscape remain dark.

With the power down, boarders at *Casa Lorna* huddled as close as they could to the fireplace fire, their fronts warm, their backs not.

Someone worked a tea kettle close enough to the flames to boil water for tea, but it did not boil.

To the west of the rhododendrons, oddly blooming with brilliant pink blossoms, the second-growth redwoods, Douglas-firs, grand firs, and tanoaks stood firm against the icy blast. The snow was heavy and took to the ground like a lover, covering all but the trails that F. Gregory had endowed and Lucy Powell had designed in a labyrinthine maze that led east and west, north and south, then and now.

And in that fury of a season that man could not warm, Williams and Earhart set out to overhear as snow fell on what was listening to them.

Kenny and Eve were on their way to the blooming rhodies to cover them if needed.

Antony was already starting up the town John Deere Snow Plow, thinking he'd wait to see if something opened up at the edge of the woods so he could get in there and open the trails to a past long dead yet never dying.

Let me back up the drive-way, say, a couple of hundred feet, to last year, the year the Celtics lost to the Knicks in the Eastern semifinals. That was the year everything in town seemed to be recessioning and a lot of people who earned by the sweat of their brow as they say were just standing around waiting to be re-trained into a service industry where they said you didn't sweat.

That was the summer that things suddenly began to open up for my good friend Frank Coletti. The way Frank put it to me was that things in the scene opened up and then the scene changed.

ABOUT THE AUTHOR

Joseph Phillip Natoli's novels include *Travels of a New Gulliver,* in which Lemuel encounters the Lilliputians, Brobdingnagians, Laputans, Balnibarbians, and the Houyhnhnms and Yahoos of the Obama years, and a *Humour noire* with counterpunches trilogy: *Get Ready to Run, Between Dog & Wolf,* and *Time is the Fire*

9 798218 606312